South Side Stories

edited by
Steve Bosak

City Stoop Press

Chicago

1993

Acknowledgements

Grateful acknowledgement from the editor to the following:

Asa Baber, "My Sister and Me" : copyright 1979 by Asa Baber. Reprinted from *Tranquillity Base and Other Stories,* published by Fiction International.

Stuart Dybek, "Flames" : copyright 1988 by Stuart Dybek. Reprinted from *Ploughshares.*

Leon Forrest, "Galloway Wheeler" : copyright 1992 by Leon Forrest. Excerpted from *Divine Dreams,* published by Another Chicago Press, Box 11223, Chicago, IL 60611.

Cover photograph by Rose Blouin

Layout, production design and typography by Thomas Swierkowski and Margaret Brennan

Many thanks to Bob Braschel at RGB Computing, Oak Brook, Illinois

The authors and editor are especially thankful to Columbia College Chicago for its support in this project; without its assistance this book would not have been possible.

Copyright 1993 City Stoop Press. All rights reserved.

Printed and bound in the United States of America.

No part of this book may be reproduced in any form without permission.

City Stoop Press
724 S. Clarence
Oak Park, Illinois 60304

Library of Congress 93-70954
ISBN 0-9627425-2-X

Contents

Stewart Dybek	**5**	*Flames*
Angela Jackson	**17**	*Plenty In Astonishment*
Asa Baber	**39**	*My Sister and Me*
Harold Holt	**61**	*Stream*
Arlene Greene	**65**	*A New Move*
Michael Fitzgerald	**83**	*Exceptional, for February*
Timothy Willis	**95**	*The Dog on the Porch*
Hoyt Fuller	**103**	*A Plundered World*
Brian Ray	**123**	*Dusk*
Leon Forrest	**135**	*Divine Days: Galloway Wheeler*
Sandra Jackson-Opoku	**143**	*Sweet Jesus Club*
Dominic Pacyga	**161**	*The South Side: A Brief History*

A Non-Introduction

Do not feel obligated to read this introduction.

You will learn nothing new about Chicago's South Side.

You will not gain a keener understanding of the why this particular geographic segment of Chicago is alternately ignored and ridiculed by the city as a whole.

But for those of you who do read on, I have another possible disappointment. I will not indulge in the Anthology Editor's typical struggle to construct some unifying/profound/yet leaky umbrella under which all the book's stories can be forced to huddle. Far from it. Style, content, subject and form are so utterly different and diverse in these pages I might as well have plucked a story from St. Louis, one from Boston and yet another from Cleveland. In fact I believe I may have done that, so scattered are many of the authors from their South Side haunts. To say anything more than these are stories from South Side authors, many set on the South Side itself, would be a bold lie.

So why this anthology? Maybe to prove to misinformed outsiders that we're not the proletariat, stereotypical lump of factory workers, janitors and project-dwellers they might imagine. Most of us speak-- and write-- perfectly amazing variations of the English language. It's not all racism, steel mills and bungalows down here. But to a man, woman and child, none of us deny there are plenty of bigots, closed factories and brick bungalows in these parts.

Everything about the South Side is perfectly obvious, until you live here.

This anthology is simply a response to the following questions, comments and observations I've had to endure over my many years as a South Sider:

> "I didn't even know this part of the city existed!" exclaimed a life-long Chicagoan, and good friend, after driving down to my flat for a Friday night poker game.

> "You live where? Isn't that near Marquette Park?" [translation: you're white and live on the South Side; therefore, you are a Nazi.]

> "But you're so far from the city!" comment many people, themselves living in Skokie, Evanston, Glenview and Rogers Park.

> "There's nothing down there, really, is there?" ask other Chicagoans. Nope. Not a thing. No wine bars, not many expensive restaurants serving nouveau American cuisine, very few health clubs or jogging trails. And we'll keep it that way until the speculators figure out that real estate prices are very attractive. I wouldn't even mention this here, for fear of planting gentrification ideas where none previously existed, but this trend has already begun in sections of Bridgeport, Beverly, Chatham and Jackson Park. Our only line of defense seems to be our bungalows themselves-- even rehabbed they still look like brick, armored-personnel carriers.

So we don't all wear babushkas, though if we did, who makes fun of Stevie Van Zant? Not all black South Siders live in poverty-- in fact the largest middle and upper-class black neighborhoods in the U.S. are on Chicago's South Side. And the factories that remain open employ some of the city's most skilled and motivated workers.

These stories will tell you all about these things, I hope, in ways you might not want to hear. If that ain't enough, get in your car and come down here some time. Drive around. Get lost.

We'll be waiting for you.

--Steven Bosak

Flames

Stewart Dybek

I met Kazmir at Mrs. Malek's. He was a couple years older than I was, though only a grade ahead of me. His blond hair was just growing back from the baldy sour they'd given him after the school nurse found lice, and the deep, white-welted scar commemorating a fall from a second-story window when he was four ran like a crack across his skull. I remembered the day at school when each class was lined against the wall in the corridor before the nurse's office. It felt like a cross between an air-raid drill and going to Confession. We filed, one at a time, into the nurse's office. Her office was dark, a black drape drawn across the window. One after another, we sat at a school desk from an eighth grade classroom with our heads slightly bowed as one of the heavyset, aproned ladies who cleaned the lunchroom sorted through our hair. The nurse stood beside her, holding a special light, following with the beam of a red bulb the trails that the lunchroom lady's fingers wove through our hair. I held my breath as if waiting for the jab of a shot. Some of the girls cried. We'd all heard how, after they'd found lice, Kazmir, struggling and cursing, had to be tied with clothesline and belts to the barber chair in the basement shop on 24th Street where old Mr. Zyunce, who could hardly understand English, gave haircuts for fifty cents. Zyunce cut a hole through the bottom of a shopping bag, fit it over Kazmir's head, and rolled the sides of the bag down to his neck, so that as he shaved Kazmir's head the hair fell into the bag. Then he daubed Kazmir's scalp with kerosene, and took the bag of blond hair into the alley to burn. Kids said you could hear the lice popping in the flames, but that was made up. Later, at Mrs. Malek's, Kazmir told me how he and his older brother, Roman, had sneaked out at night and pushed Zyunce's barber pole down the basement steps. Kazmir was light complected with blond eyelashes and pale blue eyes, and as he confided in me about knocking off the barber pole, even though he was grinning, anger burned up his neck into his face. He flushed so hotly it startled me, and I think that must have been the first time I'd ever felt the compelling force of anger I was invited to share, rather than anger directed at me.

Mrs. Malek was our babysitter for the summer, an old Bohemian woman who dressed in black and lived alone since her husband, the railroad man, had died. She may have worn black even before he died. It was a color many of the older, foreign ladies in the neighborhood gravitated to. Mr. Malek's job had been inspecting the boxcars before the freights left the yard on 17th Street, and apparently he'd had a heart attack inside one of the boxcars. Nobody missed him, and they sealed the boxcar door, and didn't find his body until they opened the door again to unload the train in Billings, Montana. By then he was frozen stiff, and had been missing long enough so that the rumor that he'd gone off on a binge and run out on Mrs. Malek had become the generally accepted truth. It was a rumor that Mrs. Malek herself seemed to confirm. When her husband failed to come home from work, she didn't even report his disappearance to the police. So, when it finally became known that Mr. Malek had died on the job, it was as if, without even trying, he had succeeded in leaving behind the feeling that the world owed him an apology. Mrs. Malek remained silent in what might or might not have been mourning, more alone than she would have been had he died in an ordinary way, while everyone else continued to discuss it. Some said that the heart attack itself hadn't killed him, that he'd probably awakened in the speeding boxcar and frozen to death; and some said it wasn't a heart attack at all, that a hobo killed him because Mr. Male had a reputation for being a son-of-a-bitch to hoboes trying to ride on what he always referred to as his trains.

They never had any kids. Mrs. Malek kept chickens in the little dirt yard behind her house on 23rd Place, all kinds-- white hens with combs the color of liver and scaly yellow legs, speckled hens with black eyes and legs to match, big red hens that seemed to turn bronze as the afternoon shadows settled in the little yard--chickens right in the middle of the city! She told us to stay away from the chickens when we went out to play, that a wild Polish rooster lived in the coop, and that he'd peck our eyes out.

Kazmir and I played in front of her house at first. I'd heard about his hot temper, but we got along from the start. And when he told me about the attack on Zyunce's barber pole, I knew we'd become friends. It was a more serious secret than one might think pushing over a barber pole would be. Zyunce's barber shop also served as a polling place. During elections the aldermen, precinct captains, and other local politicians would hang around in front, shaking hands and passing out cigars. The barber pole had come to seem like a neighborhood landmark. Besides its bold red and white stripes, a thinner blue stripe wound around it, and when it toppled, people were shocked, as if something unpatriotic had happened. They felt bad for Zyunce who already seemed so defeated by English. "What's a poor DP supposed to think about America after something like this?'' they asked.

Kazmir had another secret to tell me, a far more serious one, that it was his older brother, Roman, who pushed him out the window, almost killing him when he was four. They'd been home alone--Roman was supposed to have been watching him--and they were fooling around wrestling, and Roman had pinned him on the sill of the open window, like guys in a movie struggling at the edge of a cliff, and then Roman suddenly just let him go.

"Maybe he thought you were holding on," was all I could think of to say.

"I guess. I never asked him," Kazmir said. "I thought he had me."

When he told me that he'd never told anyone else about how he'd fallen out the window, I didn't know what to say in response. I had no secret like that to trade, and said nothing.

"I shouldn't have told you," Kazmir said, his face flushing with that quick, scalded-looking anger, and this time I couldn't tell if it was with anger for what he was remembering, or anger at me and my silence.

"Why not?" I asked.

"You might tell somebody."

"Who would I tell?"

Everyday we'd meet at Mrs. Malek's and she'd send us out to play along 23rd, a narrow little street lined with two-flats that were set in tiny front yards sunk below sidewalk level, and with three-story apartment buildings separated by gangways only wide enough for cats. Everyday we wandered a little farther from her house, widening our boundaries, and then one afternoon without even discussing it, we sneaked around the block, down the alley, and through the back gate into the tar-papered shed she called the coop. It smelled of sour grain, straw, and feathers. I held my arms ready to shield my eyes in case the rooster attacked. But there was no Polish rooster, only dark corners and intense slats of light slanting from gaps in the siding, beams of daylight that made the chicken droppings gleam the white of spilled paint. Hens clucked as if scolding outside the screen door. Kazmir grinned at me, then struck a match. He usually carried around a pocketful of matchbooks. Years later, he would found a gang called the Matchheads dedicated to torching garbage cans and junked cars, to setting trash fires behind abandoned factories, and pitching pop-bottle Molotov cocktails from overpasses late at night when the expressways were nearly deserted. All through the summer they staged hit-and-run forays as if engaged in guerrilla warfare against the city, though all they were after was to see the flames dance up incinerating the muggy night. Just as there are girls who at the onslaught of adolescence become obsessed with horses, so there are boys at the same age who worship fire. Now he was sparking matches, holding them above his head while they charred down to his fingertips, as if he were leading us with a torch through total darkness. The shed was a tangle of rusted tools and buckets, of enormous saws, rakes, hoes, shovels, an axe, a sledge hammer, a cobwebbed sickle--the only one I'd ever seen other than in pictures of the Russian flag. Rusted lanterns hung from rusted railroad spikes pounded into the beams. A row of orange crates, stuffed with straw scooped to the shape of roosting chickens, sat along the wall opposite the screen door, looking like a shipment of nests. Kazmir was flaring off whole books of matches at once. The shed felt baked and reeked of sulphur. I was afraid he was going to burn it down.

"We'd better get out of here," I whispered.

He was poking around in a corner where he'd been igniting spider webs.

"Hey, look," he whispered back. He'd pulled a crushed, canvas tarp away from a wooden washtub and there, squeaking and squirming among decomposing rags, were bald bodies not much larger than the top joint of a finger. They looked like miniature piglets with stringy, gray tails.

"What are they?" I asked.

"Must be baby rats," Kazmir said.

We'd both heard that some people in the neighborhood didn't like Mrs. Malek keeping chickens because they were afraid it attracted rats. Kazmir took a trowel from a coffee can of rusted tools and prodded, careful not to touch them with his fingers. Their eyes were closed, and their front paws looked more like miniature hands.

"I wonder if they have rabies," Kazmir said, his eyes darting around the shed.

"Rabies?" I could feel myself suddenly looking around too, for anything scurrying among the tools in the dark corners.

"You get rabies from rats," Kazmir said. "If they bite you, you have to get the shots."

"My father had to get the shots," I said, recalling my father's story of how, as a boy, he went every day for fourteen days to St. Anthony's Hospital for rabies shots after his landlady's dog bit him. The landlady had told his mother, my grandmother, that the dog was a watchdog and that my father shouldn't have bothered it, that she didn't want her watchdog locked up in the dog pound, and that if they told the doctors whose dog it was they'd have to move out of the building. My grandmother had come over on the boat from

Poland, as my father put it, and didn't know the score yet, but she knew that cheap flats for a woman with six kids weren't that easy to find, and so my father went for the shots, and every day when he came home my grandmother would give him a warm sponge bath to ease the soreness. The worst part, my father said, was that the whole time he knew the landlady's dog didn't have rabies, it was just mean.

"When his butt got sore they gave him the shots in the stomach," I told Kazmir.

"He shouldn't have told them his butt was sore," Kazmir said. He'd pried the lid off an old paint can, and I watched as he carefully troweled the bald bodies into the can. Then, with a long-handled blade for scraping ice from sidewalks, he churned them up. The can tipped when he tried to get the blade out, and he had to step on the can in order to work the scraper loose, then he jammed the blade into the dirt floor of the shed. I didn't try to help him, and he didn't ask. Outside the screen door, the hubbub of chickens that had seemed to vanish into silence while Kazmir was chopping with the scraper, now seemed louder and more hysterical than before. Kazmir went over to the crates, picked out a couple of brown eggs from the straw, cracked them on the rim of the can, and threw them in, shells and all. Then he pissed in the can, and we took the whole mess outside into the yard to see what the chickens would do.

And when he spilled it into the dirt, the only thing I'd ever seen move faster than those chickens was the whoosh of gasoline the summer before when a tramp tried to burn the weeds along the railroad embankment on 25th. The men who worked for the railroad were supposed to keep the weeds cut back from the tracks, but in late summer, when the weeds sprouted tall, they usually burned them in a hot, quick, intense blaze which in moments reduced the jungle of the embankment into a charred stubble that looked like melted plastic. A bunch of us kids always stood around watching the weeds burn, but this time the railroad men gave a hobo whiskey money to do it, while they sat drinking beer from sweaty quart bottles. He poured what they told him was kerosene along both sides of the tracks, slopping it over the weeds, then struck a match and tossed it. A balled blast of orange thumped up and hit him where he stood between the rails surrounded by hip-high weeds that were now even taller flames. The railroad men jumped up, both laughing and hollering for him to get the hell out of there, and between the flames the hobo stood enveloped in bright air that wavered as if it were bending or melting in the heat, an astonished look on his face, the shoulders of his suit coat smoldering, and then suddenly his astonishment turned into a look of pleading terror, he screamed and, throwing his arm across his eyes as if playing blind man's bluff, he ran through the fire, pitching forward and rolling down the embankment so that it was impossible to tell if it was dust or smoke surrounding him as he thrashed. Chickens were all around us, screeching and pecking and gobbling as if they'd gone crazy, and Mrs. Malek in a rush of black skirts was running out with a broom, yelling in Bohemian, while Kazmir and I stood among the beating wings, trying to kick dirt over the guts as if stamping out flames.

Maroon

for Anthony Dadaro, 1946-58

Stewart Dybek

A boy is bouncing a ball off a brick wall after school. The bricks had been painted maroon a long time ago. Steady as a heartbeat the ball rebounds oblong, hums, sponges back round. A maroon Chevy goes by.

Nothing else. This street's deserted: a block-long abandoned factory, glass from the busted windows on the sidewalk mixed with brown glass from beer bottles, whiskey pints. Sometimes the alkies drink here. Not today.

Only the ball flying between sunlit hands and shadowed bricks and sparrows brawling in the dusty gutters. The entire street turning maroon in the shadow of the wall, even the birds, even the hands.

He stands waiting under a streetlight that's trying to flicker on. Three guys he's never seen in the neighborhood before, coming down the street, carrying crowbars.

Belly Button

Stewart Dybek

What was it about the belly button that connected it to the Old Country?

Perhaps, Busha's concern for its cleanliness. Those winter bath nights, windows and mirrors steamed as if we were simmering soup, my hands "wrinkled as prunes," the slippery bathwater sloshing as I stepped from the tub into her terrycloth embrace.

Outside, night billowed like the habits of nuns through vigil lights of snow. Krakow was only blocks away, just past Goldblatt's darkened sign. Bells tolled from the steeple of St. Kasmir's, over the water towers and smokestacks, over the huddled villages and ghettoes of Chicago.

And at the center of my body, Busha's rosary-pinched fingers picked at that knotted opening that promised to lead inward, but never did.

Plenty In Astonishment

Angela Jackson

Anything was liable to come cruising down that wide street. A little old white man in white pants, shirt, apron, and a chef's hat as large as he, would come stepping out of a giant red wiener and wave at us as the wiener-in-a-bun-on-wheels went gliding by. Leaving us children gape-mouthed and joyous at the sight of such miracles of commerce. And the adults, well...

"There go Little Oscar," Aunt Jamie said. "I tell you about the time I like to choke on one of them weanies?" Nobody answered because we knew Aunt Jamie was just beginning a conversation with herself. If we didn't interrupt, we'd be in luck. We could eavesdrop.

"That's what I get for trying to eat something that look like that. Nasty thing. Got a little man walking out of it instead of the other way around. What they gon do next?"

"Ain't no tellin," she squeezed her mouth tight so we'd know no conjecture was coming from her. To prophecy what the city would do next would be like second guessing a god whose specialty was cosmic caprice. The universe here was so tilted and magical our street was called Plenty. It was a street of working and wished-they-were-working adults, and play-squealing children. On Plenty the high, thrilling laugh of the child scribbled in the air next to the raucous grunts and cries from the huge pens of corraled animals that rumbled by on the way to the Stockyards.

Jubilant, we watched, anticipating the rank, animal reek that would escape through the slats of the trucks. The odor of bovine excretions, the harsh, high smelling and bottomless aroma of their death sensing fear would be cause for us to hold our noses, gag, and cackle with glee. Perverse in the thick of impending slaughter, our hearts would race defiantly. All that dying going right by us.

One bright day a bull broke through the slats of the slaughter truck. He leapt like heavy, hot smoke onto the pavement; his forelegs buckling at the impact. Then he lumbered back to balance and thundered out of the street and through the little silver gate into the little churchyard of the church that was a clapboard house. Aunt Jamie was standing on the church steps, the rickety porch stairs, talking to the Reverend's wife about how it was permissible for the preacher's wife to wear a scarlet blouse, when the bull came by, pawing at the foot of the steps, blowing strings of hot snot through big, raw-red nostrils.

The Reverend's wife stepped backwards through the doorway and closed the door in one movement. Aunt Jamie looked into the bull's eyes. "Shoo," she said, rolling the air with the swath of red material she would whip into a blouse for the preacher's wife.

"Shoo," she repeated and waved the fabric. Then she said, "Oh, the devil! Get on way from here."

The bull pawed two holes into the cement pathway in front of the steps. In a keyhole of time the world ran quiet and came out a key of light. Everybody waited for Aunt Jamie to die. Now the only inevitable event in the middle of cosmic surprise. But just when the bull tucked his head into his huge chest and aimed his horns at Aunt Jamie, the truck drivers came with their prods and rope and wrestled and shoved him back into the truck, up a plank and into a crack between more stinking, soon-to-be-dead beasts. The truck that was always a closed mystery to us gaped open like a mouth, with a dirty wooden tongue sticking out onto the street. The mouth was full of meat, moving and sweating. We children were struck dumb to see so much heavy animal flesh, to smell the breath-smothering stench. We watched, and no one dared say a word, even while Aunt Jamie conversed with herself about how stupid she was to be egging that bull on when she thought she was running him away. Her with a red rag in her hand.

Mama said later the bull had panicked. He sensed he was on a straight course to the killing floor, so he did what he could. He ran for his life. And he was ready to take the whole world with him.

Aunt Jamie considered this, "When you think about it, it makes sense."

But nobody really *thought* about it. So it never made sense. Especially not to me when Nicky read to me from "Ripley's Believe It Or Not" that bulls don't even see red. Any color will do. It's not the color of the cloth but everything else that drives them wild.

Before the bull, or after it, Folger's put promises on the billboard just off Plenty. It promised to bring a mountain to Chicago. I kept waiting and waiting, but the only thing that came was coffee and I didn't like that, so something inside me kept waiting for the mountain to come right down our street. Until it did come.

They moved in in the middle of the night.

We heard the quick footsteps of children in the dark. We, my brother Nicodemus and I, scrambled to the foggy window to see the figures of two grown white men rumbling through the rain. They carried a ripped-seated couch teetertottering between them. We could make out the image of a woman through our dark glass. Unclear though she was, she seemed forlorn. Her arms were wrapped around her chest like a straight jacket. She clutched something close. We couldn't see what because we wouldn't look hard enough. We weren't interested in her or the two men who carried the tilting couch.

We saw children and we were enchanted. A girl in a light dress was dancing in the backyard next door. A boy was dragging something heavy through the backdoor of the vacant first floor apartment where my friend, Alberta, used to live. We used to fight one day, then play the next. The day she moved so her daddy could work in the steel mills we were playing. So I didn't have anger or a grudge to fill her space. Now a girl's dress -- what I could see like ghost skin of a gone friend -- flashed as pale colors do in darkness. She was small beside the monkeycigar tree whose roots grew deep on our side of the fence, but whose breadth was so generous and indiscriminant the tree threw its many cigared arms wide onto the neighboring property.

It was one o'clock in the Saturday morning and white people were moving next door to us. Our child eyes were open illegally because both of our parents had gone to the church dinner dance. Now they widened in astonishment, while Aunt Jamie's narrowed in suspicion. There was only one explanation: they were poor. That had to be the logic that their sad belongings verified. They were poorer than the Southern soil that hawked and spit them clean down the highway. Poorer than the dirt that clung to their license plates: Mississippi. Aunt Jamie's gaze pierced the darkness til she'd made that out. Mississippi.

"White trash," Aunt Jamesora said. "Nothing but poor white trash." She bit the thread and shook out the newly hemmed skirt. She was up working. Working. As always. Mary Cecelia stood shivering in her slip. Aunt Jamie's breath blowing on her bare brown back.

I was at the window, waiting for another glimpse of the girl who was moving into my friend's house. The men went in last, after the woman and children had long been inside.

"Anytime white people come to live amongst colored people who ain't got no money, you know they scraping the bottom of the bottom of the barrel." Aunt Jamie added two cents to her first two cents. She said this definitely, like it was four.

"We just as good as them," I interrupted, ready to defend my race, even if it meant she'd notice I wasn't asleep. Just like Ida B. Wells the city named a project after.

My sister, Mary-Cecilia, shot me a warning look. She rubbed her bare shoulders because Aunt Jamie had sent a chill through the room. I didn't say anything.

"I know we as good as them. I know we better," Aunt Jamie was hitting Mary-Cecilia's skirt with the iron. She hit the I at the same time. "I know this, and I hope *you* know it too." She hit the *you*. "I'm talking from their minds now. They have to live amongst Negroes. And to they mind, they in Hell. No place worse to go." She whipped the skirt until it snapped. Making a crack in the air, dividing it like the Red Sea. I was seasick with excitement. White people had moved next door. Plenty swerved and tilted. Next door there was a girl my age.

After three days, during which I climbed the monkeycigar tree and spied across into the next yard for some sign of life besides the two men who went in and out in rough-dry clothes and thin wet hair to an old dented car that still had Mississippi mud on the wheels, the little girl next door came out to play. Nicodemus was, as usual, telling me to get down out of that tree before I came down the hard way. He stopped, mouth open at the sight of that back door opening and a girl coming out.

"See," I said to him triumphantly.

He just watched her and, deciding she was just a girl and a scrawny one at that, he went away. I awaited the approach of a possible friend.

She didn't say anything to me. She turned and watched the woman come out of the door with a pail of wet clothes in her hands.

As if on cue, my mother came outside with a basket of wet clothes. I ran to her so I could hand her things.

Soon Mama and the white woman, each minding her own business, without a thought of the other, were hanging up men's underwear. The sun was high and accommodating to their task. My mother looked over her shoulder and pulled a clothespin out of her mouth. As if she were seeing her for the first time, she looked over at the woman who kept her eyes on her husband's long johns.

"Good morning!" my mother hollered over the fence. It was her street after all. The woman smiled nervously. She bent her head a little in response. Mama opened her mouth to say more; looking at me, she thought better of it. She finished hanging up the laundry. Then she just stood looking up at the sky because she loved it so. My mother named me Regina after herself. She named me Regina Caeli, Queen of Heaven, because she put her stock in a God who was benevolent and omnipresent, but whose will ran truest to form in Heaven. She wished me well, but Queen of Heaven was too heavy for me to carry around everyday. Everybody called me Peaches.

The little girl sauntered over to the fence. I put down the stick I was pretending to be drawing with, having wiped the dampness from the clean wet clothes onto my dress. I inched over to the same place on my side of the fence.

The new girl looked at me out of the corner of her eye. "I saw you move in," I said. "You went in the house right behind yo couch."

"I was born on that couch." She said her words like the people on TV who said Nigra and that other word we got a whipping for saying. She talked just like the people on the news.

But this little girl was smiling. Lots of space between her bad teeth. She was jumpy, she was so happy to be outside. Her dress was thin as toilet tissue, and it hung on her just like on a hanger. The cotton twitched and skipped when she did.

"My name Peaches. What's yo name?" I asked her, moving my head up and down to follow her.

The question put another skip in her. "My name Nina." By the time she finished her name, I thought it was Niner, and nine syllables long.

We were the same age, though I was bigger. And I had all my teeth. I wasn't big for my age. Nina was just puny. "Po," my Aunt Jamesora said. Her eyes were supposed to be brown, but they were red. Little red eyes that moved around a lot real quick so she could see a lick before it hit her. She settled them on me, considering. Then she started acting like Bette Davis in "Jezebel." Her head tilted to the side. The cheek with the pretty dimple in it turned up. Her little lips, the pinkest things I'd ever seen.

"You like my hair?" she asked me. It was just laying there. It was brown, but it was supposed to be gold. I didn't like it, but I said I did just to be nice. She expected it. Or maybe she just hoped real hard.

I didn't like her runny nose either, but I ignored it. My mother expected this. You're not supposed to make people feel bad about themselves.

"My daddy gonna buy me a barrette," she announced. Her little red eyes were full of lights. And the teeny dimple in her cheek was like a deep star.

Later, the same day, Aunt Jamie said a barrette was about the only thing her daddy could afford to buy her on General Assistance. This disgusted Aunt Jamie for a white person not to be rich. "In this day and age, he ain't got no excuse not to have found himself something. He got the *first* credential." Her hands were busy with the hot curlers. She was bumping curls all over Mary-Cecilia's head. The newly straightened hair she kept pushing to the side, as she sectioned off another patch of pressed hair to wind inside the smoking curlers. She shivered the curlers inside the roll of hair, then slid them out, leaving the bumper curl intact behind.

"Hold your ear," she ordered my sister as she caught up a few strands for a side curl that would curve around Mary Cecelia's ear. It was a pixie cut everybody said was so cute on her.

Mama was snapping beans, and I was helping her. She'd always resnap mine, because mine were too big. I was hoping she'd tell me to quit helping her, but she didn't.

Aunt Jamie was telling the story. "You know how they come to get an apartment on this street?" Aunt Jamie's voice was sly, anticipating Mama's curiosity.

"Naw, "Mama said, her mouth tilting up already. "Somebody Down South told them about *plenty* streets with nice apartments."

Mama laughed til tears jumped in her eyes and ran out the corners. Aunt Jamie laughed because Mama did, and because her joke had caught even her by surprise.

"I guess if somebody told them this was the land of milk and honey, they'd a tried to move in Wanzer's. *Wanzer's on milk is like Sterling on silver.*" Aunt Jamie closed with the advertising slogan and this cracked them up even more. They giggled for a long time, quieted down, then bust out laughing again when the joke knocked a funny bone or its echo did. Suddenly, at last, Mama wiped her eyes and sighed, "ah-ho," and I knew that meant the laughing was over. But Aunt Jamie knew more. She set the curlers on the stove-eye and rested her hands. Just for a minute, did nothing with her hands, but lay them on Mary-Cecilia's shoulders.

"You know what, Red?" That's what she called my mother. Red. Red Fields.

"What?" Red, my mother, said.

"They from Money, Mississippi." She didn't just look at Mama now, she communicated with her eyes. Mama's mouth fell open.

"That place they killed that boy?" Mama asked more to say it than to ask.

"Uh huh."

"Were they in on it?" My mother's voice was very deep now.

"Your guess is as good as mine."

Mama began to snap and resnap beans furiously. Aunt Jamie was twirling her curlers, blowing on them. Then Aunt Jamie got the devil in her and threw her head back in a deep laugh that flew into a shriek. "Ain't that nothing. They from Money, and they ain't got none." She laughed til she coughed. The next part came out dry. "Ain't got no sense neither." she said. "Moving around here. Instead of takin' theyselves up around that Uptown where the po white and the Iranians stay."

"Money, money, money, money, money." That's the way Aunt Jamie sealed the case against the white people. Until it popped open again, like a Pandora's box with an ornery lid spring.

For a time Mama's eyes narrowed like Aunt Jamie's when they talked about the white people next door. Til one day I heard Mama tell Aunt Jamie how under the weather the woman was looking lately, sickly, like she was having a bad time of it with a man or a child. "She look like she's expecting," Mama told Aunt Jamie. I was eavesdropping in the doorway. When Mama said this, I tilted my head into the kitchen, so I could see my mother's eyes. They were wider and softer. Misty. They'd been talking about something else, and Mama'd dropped that in, because by then talking about the white people was like talking about the weather.

One storm blew out of a rumor. Someone said the family called themselves Gordon, but their *real* name was Wallace. This was irrevocable indignity. A source of heartburn. Every time Mr. Gordon-Wallace stood in his shabby, dingy clothes in the doorway of the rented back apartment, the state of Alabama stood with him. The Mississippi on the license plate was some devious red herring, so we wouldn't know that whatever state was in the news was the one they were from. His wife was Dixie. There was no mistaking that. Someone had heard the man call her that. Someone else said they had seen her bloomers on the line, and they were cut from the Confederate flag. The second somebody was a lie, but it didn't matter because everybody knew the idea was true and axiomatic. Yet, even that storm blew through Plenty after a time. And their name was Gordon after all. Yet the deep, sulky feelings that the story unsettled still floated in the atmosphere, because a change in spirit is more permanent than a change in appearance.

Plenty had been changed when the city tore down one side of the street to make way for the expressway. The large mansion where Mount Tabor Missionary Baptist Church held its teas, the grocery store, the butcher shoppe, the drug store, the candy store, the cleaners, all commerce, all establishments of industry were gone. A half of our world suddenly wiped clear. In its place, grass grew when and where no one asked it to. Time walked backwards before our eyes and primeval insects buzzed out of the beginning of time before humanity; quick rabbits magically propogated (like faith), pricked up their ears and shot their heads up above the grass, then disappeared. I caught my breath at a glimpse of a rabbit, loving them involuntarily because they were small and consequently at the mercy of everything. I thought they ran cagily, expertly, just ahead of murder and entrapment.

But the boys, equally quick and flexible, strategized their capture. My brothers Luke and Nicodemus caught five rabbits. They built a cage for them in the backyard. They discussed what to do with the rabbits. I stood near the wire enclosure and watched the rabbits urinate. They were not nearly as attractive and not at all smart alecky like Bugs Bunny, but they fascinated me.

Luke wanted to start a rabbit factory, and sell rabbits wholesale to Kroger's, A&P, and Certified. Nicodemus didn't know what he wanted to do with them. He just wanted to keep them. To feed them and watch them. I was with Nicky. I watched the rabbits shivering and looking stupid.

"What ya'll got?" Niner hollered at us from the next yard because she was a friend of mine.

Luke and Nicodemus wouldn't speak to her. Not because she was white, but because she was a girl. Most of all they wouldn't speak because she was a white girl.

Then the boy came out who hadn't been out since they'd moved in. He looked like a hungry, miniature vampire, bloodless and sick. He ran right over to Nina and started dragging her off of the fence that she had climbed up on to get a better look.

"I wanna see the bunny rabbits," Nina cried. "I wanna see --" But he cut her off when he hammered her fingers with his white knuckled fists to make her turn loose the fence. She yelped like a little dog that's been kicked, and fell back into his skinny arms.

He dragged her across the yard, that same thin dress all hiked up in front so we could see her baggy panties that must have belonged to her mama, and her belly thin-skinned like the underside of a fish. Once he got her inside, he slammed the door. "Goddog," Nicky marveled. "You see how he did his sister?" There was awe in Nicky's voice and a kind of hurt because the vampire-boy hadn't said a word to any of us. And he was Nicky's age.

"I'd like to see you try that on Peaches," Luke joked and looked at me for the reaction he got.

"Yeah, try it," I dared them.

"Oh, my goodness, girl," Nicky said with disgust. "We let you help us feed the rabbits, didn't we?"

"Plus, we will give you the honor of cleaning out the cage," Luke put his arm around my neck. I shoved his arm off.

"You can do it," I told him as I ran away.

"You the laziest girl alive," Luke said.

"Sticks and stones may break my bones," I yelled back, "but names---"

"----gone make you mad," Luke finished so he and Nicky could crack up and make their voices deeper than they were.

The rabbits became the center of our half a world. We got up in the morning and fed them. We changed their water. And once or twice I did clean the cage. The rabbits were a source of boundless expectancy and excitement. Soon white people next door were normal and boring. Unworthy of assiduous examination. Three of the rabbits began to change. They grew heavier and slower. Luke said they were "rabbettes" and they were going to have babies.

"They just like poor people," Luke said. "They can't make any money. All they can make is more of themselves."

We awaited the birth of a new generation of rabbits. So obsessed was I with the coming of the infants that I got up at night to watch the bunnies in case I could catch them giving birth. One night when summer was ending everybody but the Gordons was gathered outside on the front stoop watching the boys singing under the lamppost, "Money, I need some money. Oh, baby. I must pay the milkman, pay the grocery boy and postman too. You don't seem to realize...I need money" in a rich, complicated harmony where one voice ended and another began on top of it. And everybody present was audience and recipient, because music was money then, and in these moments our parents were well paid.

I sneaked away from the crowd of grown folks sipping ice water, music, and beer and the kids playing games and imitating the singers. I slipped through the dark gangway and went to the back to watch the rabbits. But someone else was there before me.

The Gordon boy was hunched near the cage feeding the rabbits crusts of bread. He was talking to them in a gentle boy voice. The rabbits accepted the bits of food he slipped through the wire. "These people don't know nothing bout no rabbits," he cooed to our pets. "These city people don't know a thing about what a rabbit needs."

I didn't say anything. Didn't make a sound. I just slipped back up front. When my mother asked me where I'd been, I told her I had to use the bathroom.

The next day was Friday, and Aunt Jamie had gone fishing early in the morning to bring something back for dinner. She wasn't Catholic, but since she lived with us she ate what we ate. And we ate fish on Friday. I wasn't sure I liked fish when they were alive. They wiggled too much. And catfish didn't look like fish, they looked like wiggling devils with whiskers. So I stayed outside, because I didn't like catfish. I watched the rabbits instead and waited for the birthing. I hadn't seen Nina much since the rabbits had first become the center of our lives. I had seen her brother only that night. And the mother I saw less and less. She had spoken to me a little while. But shē gave that up. She came out the door this afternoon and just walked with a little bag of garbage in a brown bag to the alley. She was looking real bad. And walking like somebody had shot her in the stomach. She took my mind off the rabbits for a while.

I had been reading Nancy Drew books, so I was a detective. I followed her into the alley.

There she sat on a little piece of concrete. She sat with her legs open. Sunlight went between her legs. A great darkness was shielded and revealed. She sat pantieless and hopeless in the alley. Her sanitary napkin humped over her private place like a cotton hill hiding a valley.

"She just got on a Kotex too," I turned up my broad nose and told it to Aunt Jamie when she came out with a soiled newspaper full of fish entrails. Fish guts, slick catfish skin, and useless bones were wrapped in the day old *Sun-Times* and jammed into the brown Kroger's bag. She waded through flies to open the garbage can.

"Miz Gordon," I told Aunt Jamie, "she ain't got on no panties. And she on her period too." I reported like I was not to blame. I placed myself outside the circle of Aunt Jamie's wrath even as I called it down.

Aunt Jamie stopped in the middle of a hand-stroke. Flies flew away from the stillness. She saw the woman then, sitting with her head on her arm and her legs too wide open.

"Woman, if you don't get on away from here, gapping your legs all over the place in front of these children. If you don't get out of my face, you better."

Mrs. Gordon woke up from her pain. She shook her head like a child who has been falsely accused. Her dirty hair swung around like greased whips. Her eyes filled with tears; she opened them wider to take in the image of Aunt Jamesora with a swarm of flies circling her wrist where her hand still rested on the garbage lid, holding it down with all her strength.

"Oh, God," the woman cried.

"He don't talk to you til you put on some clothes. That's been the rules since Adam and Eve," Aunt Jamie said coolly. Her voice stern and matter-of-fact.

"Why he put me on this cross, then walk away from me?" The woman hiccuped and doubled over like the whole lower half of her body was killing her.

"Damn," Aunt Jamie said like she was mad at the woman for making her do something she didn't mean to do. She walked over to the woman and sat down beside her. She put her arm around the woman's shoulders. "Close your legs," she said simply.

Then Aunt Jamie shooed me away. "Get on away from here, Peaches," she commanded me. "Go, girl, go see if your mama come home from work yet."

That night the rabbits disappeared, and the next day was the big storm about the Gordons. One of the boys said the Gordons stole those rabbits and ate them heads and all. The boy said they really stole them so they could get a rabbit's foot to improve their luck so they wouldn't have to live with Negroes anymore. I don't know which part of the story stirred up the most wind, but the whole thing blew through the neighborhood, and people were mad.

That night we heard shots, and we all flew to the back. We could see the fire coming out of the end of Mr. Gordon's shotgun.

"Get away from here. I'm going to call the sheriff on you!" Mr. Gordon howled. His voice carrying through the darkness far farther than the fire that blazed from the barrels of his rifle.

"Don't go out there, Carthage," my mama pleaded with my father. "He's got a gun."

But my father went anyway.

I watched at the window. I could hear the two men talking like two shadows in the darkness. When Papa came back, he said that somebody had knocked on Mr. Gordon's back door and then run. I wondered why if Mr. Gordon had a gun he didn't just go hunting for rabbits instead of stealing them. The next night he did. By then we hated Mr. Gordon because we knew he must have stolen our rabbits. So because I hated him I watched him as conscientiously as I'd watched the rabbits that I loved.

I saw Mr. Gordon go loping in the dark. His rifle at his hip.

"Mr. Gordon going hunting," I announced to the house. "He ought to shoot that ugly wife of his." Luke looked up from *Negro Digest*.

"He ought to shoot hisself while he shooting ugly. He mean. She at least halfway nice." I was thinking of Nina too.

"Nice nasty. Don't wear no underwear," Luke said.

"How you know?" I asked him.

"I got my spies."

"Been looking up under that white woman's dress, Luke?" Aunt Jamie said more than asked. We hadn't heard her come into the kitchen where I was washing dishes, and we were all listening to the radio. "Your eyes gone get infected and run snot."

"Jamie. Please." Mama begged from the dining room where she was counting out tuition money for school next week.

Aunt Jamie kept quiet for a minute til she knew Mama was counting money again. Then she drew her eyes into squinting slits. "You seen those glasses Mr. Magoo have on," she whispered to Luke. "That's gone be you."

Luke got mad. "It ain't hardly gone be me," he denied. I wasn't looking.

Nina was out of prison with a barrette in her hair. She was dressed up and even had on socks. It was my first day of school. Nina was going to public school. She'd gone to register, and she'd been a big hit with the white teacher. But everybody knew that even before Nina told it.

When Nicky and I came home, we were in our uniforms. He was very handsome in his white shirt and blue tie. I had on my blue jumper and two white ribbons on the short braids in my hair.

Nina was clean, but her nose was still brimming. Her eyes red and soft with the compliments she'd received at school. My father, Carthage Fields, had told us a female rabbit was called a doe, and a male one was a buck. I was thinking of a doe, and Nina's daddy and what he had done to our rabbits. Nicky was standing there looking impatient, because he wanted to go upstairs and change and show me how to be in fourth grade. Nina smiled and showed her dimple. Suddenly, she was Jezebel like on the day we'd first met. She swung her body from side to side, and when she swung, her eyes on Nicky all the while, a rabbit's foot on a chain worked its way out of her waistband. I saw red.

"You like my hair?" she asked Nicky. Nicky just glared at her with her snotty nose. Offended. Then he went upstairs, stopping on the landing to call my name once. But I wasn't listening to his voice. I had other voices in my head now. Raucous, rich and mighty with insult.

I threw down my schoolbooks and started a loud serenade. "Yo mama don't wear no drawers/ I saw her when she took em off/ She hung them on the line/ The sun refused to shine."

All the lights went out of Nina's eyes. And her chest huffed up. Something came out of her from deep inside.

"Nigger," Niner said. And licked the by-now-running snot from her upper lip. When I hit her she must have bitten her tongue because blood came out of her mouth and snot out of her nose. My knuckles were sticky. She made an old howl of pain, spit blood on me, and ran.

I chased her over the fence, through the backyard and up to her back door. She ran in and slammed the door in my face.

Everything was quiet. All sound had run through the keyhole into that house. She was in that house that wasn't even hers. I was by myself in the yard.

I kicked around the monkeycigar tree on their side for a little time. Then I climbed back over my fence. I could feel her blood on my cheek now. It was heavy and sticky. I wiped my knuckles on my jumper, but I wouldn't touch her blood, so I pulled a big leaf from the monkeycigar tree and wiped the blood off my cheek with the wide leaf. Then I pulled another leaf off and used that too. Then another one. And another. I was just sitting there wiping, scrubbing my face with the leaves.

Nicky came back downstairs and looked at me squatting on the ground and scouring my cheek like a burnt pot. A pile of leaves between my knees.

"Peaches, what's wrong with you? Why you putting that green all over your face?" Then my eyes filled up and my shoulders started to go up and down, my lips shook, but I didn't talk.

They moved out in the middle of the night, the day before the sheriff came to evict them for not paying rent. That is what Aunt Jamie said. Somehow she'd gathered the pieces of the story from different people and stitched what she had into logical garment.

"The man say he couldn't find no work. Just drive around all day with his po self feeding that big ole ugly car. The woman didn't have any money, because the man refused to give her any of the welfare check money. The children were starving. Eating bread and gravy, because he say beans is what niggers eat. People supposed to have meat. They were hungry. The woman say she'd already lost one baby."

"Poor thing," Mama said, her eyes cast down as she darned Mary-Cecelia's white uniform socks.

Aunt Jamie had made homemade ice cream. She filled bowls and finished her story. We looked at the bowls, but no one was really anxious for it.

"The boy was sickly and refused to eat the rabbits, and his mother was afraid that he would die too. She beat that child with everything she had in her until he took that meat in his mouth and chewed and swallowed it. They probably wouldn't have starved to death. Just got sick and died from that. Or just been sick and stupid."

I was sitting in the big chair looking out the front window at the big field where the expressway would be soon. The grasses swayed to and fro. And I knew rabbits were skipping and running where we couldn't see. In the cool of night hunching close to rocks for the remaining warmth of the sun, like my daddy said they did.

"That's why I gave her one of the kids' rabbits," Mama's voice was quiet and sweet and private -- the way it is in the confessional. Once I went with her and, waiting outside collecting my sins for words in my mouth, listened to the tone of her atonement, not specific sins. Her voice turning over like her heart, making itself new, in a painful bewildered repentance.

We all looked at her, but nobody said anything. Just looked at her quiet face, the cheekbones high as heaven. Her eyes intent upon her work. We watched her hands then, tense and quick. Her stitches so tiny nobody but the fine-eyed would make them out. My sister would feel no telling bump at her heel that would make repair too much a part of her walk. Mama's quiet voice came again. "I only gave her one. Now he shouldn't have taken the rest." Her voice so hot, she stopped her hands and spooned the ice cream into her mouth. "He shouldn't have done that; that was wrong." Her voice thick with the icy sweetened cream, regret, and anger.

I looked away from her. Plenty was all my eyes would hold. I squeezed into a corner of the window, my cheek smashed against the glass, trying to see far down the avenue. As far as possible. I could see way to Comiskey Park, and tonight there were fireworks. It was Labor Day. Night. Little bits and strings of light ran around in the sky, and everybody but Mama gathered at the window to watch. Everybody breathed "Oooh," and "Ahhhh," and looked up until their necks got stiff. Then the fireworks died. And the sky was dark and silent again. Everybody else went away from the window, but I kept looking, because the darkness knew everything, and I didn't want to look down and see anything missing from our street.

When, in answer to her inquiry, I said I didn't want ice cream, Aunt Jamie decided I was sick. Then I *was* a little sick in the pit of my stomach. That's why I came away from the window and crowded up under my mother's elbow and watched her fingers go inside the sock and turn it inside out to do her tiny work. I smelled her arm, my face so close her skin was dark as the earth, and like the earth after a big downpour it always smelled so clean, generous, and just washed.

My Sister And Me

Asa Baber

For fifteen you would say I am advanced. This would get no argument from me because I am proud of my size and I like people to notice me. I am six feet tall but no creep. My sister's girlfriends all say they would date me, and more than once I have gone out with them after their show.

I am not implying that I am a great lover, but I am advanced in all areas, even though my scores are none of your business.

Suzy got this crazy idea one night when we were at Trader Vic's. I thought it was the rum talking, so I cooled it and didn't argue at first, which was a mistake because when she gets an idea, she keeps it. She doesn't have many, but she keeps the ones she's got. I was with Dawn that night and Suzy was with Mr. Loeb, who is a slob but pays the bills.

"What you need is a good school, Jerry," Suzy said.

Mr. Loeb picked it up like a cue. "A boy has to be well educated these days or he'll go nowhere."

"I keep telling him that. He's got all sorts of big-shot ideas and he won't listen to me."

"He thinks he can go on like this with me paying for him?" Mr. Loeb decided to do something big. "Suzy, you get this boy in school. Already he has missed a year and is running around Chicago like an adult with no responsibilities. You take him and find him the most expensive school you can get. A check I give you--four thousand bucks I give you for the first year. Like a son he is to me, and I want him to have the best."

He wrote out the check and handed it to Suzy, who tried to act like it was something that happened every day.

All I could do was gobble egg roll and suck rum through my straw. Dawn and me had ordered one of those big drinks with a gardenia floating in it. I knew she was shook up about the check, not because she wanted the money or anything, but because she didn't want to lose me.

Now don't get psychoanalytic about it. Dawn is as old as Suzy, almost twenty-eight, and we had a few things going which are none of your business, but mostly it was just that we could talk to each other.

Dawn danced in the same show as my sister, but she had a lead number, and she was intelligent in a crazy way.

Like before Mr. Loeb had upstaged us all, she had been talking about Machiavelli, which was part of the reading assignment she had given me.

Suzy looked at the check a couple of times. She tried to cry, but it was tough while she read the account number and the date and made sure everything was OK. Then she cried real good and excused herself for a minute.

Mr. Loeb tried to go out with her, but she stood up to her six feet two and just pushed him back down like the shrimp he was.

So he talked big to me about initiative and character and how he'd made it in sausages and refrigerated meats. When Suzy came back we had sweet-sour pork and fried rice and pressed duck. Dawn and me ate with chopsticks.

It was too late to have more drinks, so we went right over to The Frolics in a cab because the girls have to be there half an hour before show time.

Mr. Loeb went to his table and I went backstage with the girls.

Most guys my age would probably play with themselves at the thought of going backstage with the line at The Frolics, but then they have not been going back there for ten years. It was for me a family affair. I knew all the girls and they had known my parents before they were killed, so it was no big deal.

That is not to say I didn't keep my eyes open. Most of the time I was sneaking around the band.

I always bugged Sonny during rehearsals and got him to teach me something about the drums. He said I'd probably be about as good a drummer as a white man could be, and I could run through the basic flams and paradiddles pretty well. Sonny let me sit in every once in a while.

This particular night I didn't even care because it would all be over and I'd be back in school soon. Besides, his eyes were glassy. I knew Sonny was on the stuff and wouldn't talk to anyone.

I sat there and listened to the show out front. Mac was on with his Irish-Jew jokes I'd heard a hundred times, and the poor johns were laughing it up, as if that would bring on the girls.

Nothing sounds funny backstage.

No, that's not right. If somebody goofs out front, then I'd laugh my fool head off. Sometimes Mac was a little stewed and he'd screw up a punch line or something, and then I'd laugh. Dawn came over with a book. Every night she gave me a new book to read. That's the best kind of education.

"School will be good for you, Jerry."

"I don't think so."

"This is no life for a kid. I'm bad for you too."

"Don't start that. I'm not a kid."

"In some ways you are."

"How many guys my age are reading Walter Lippmann?"

"Don't be silly. You aren't in the system, and that's what hurts. You read comics in the system, you win. You read Lippmann outside, you lose. There's my cue."

She stood up and shook her arms like they were noodles. Dawn never talked about it, but I don't think she liked to strip in front of those guys. She had a fast number, you know, lots of business, and she always came offstage out of breath and tired, but cool still, sweet-smelling like Jasmine. Some of the girls, like Candy, smelled like hogs after a set. They were supposed to be sexy because they got sweaty and basic, but they always reminded me of wrestlers.

The night was shot.

Suzy tried to make it big and gay, like we had discovered the secret to cancer or something. But I knew that she'd given notice, and that the next day we'd head for school. So I sulked, which is the right of any fifteen-year-old. They played like it was a joyous time, like I'd just been circumcised, and we hit the spots after the show.

It was useless. We dropped Dawn at her apartment and Mr. Loeb stayed in our living room while Suzy made a fuss about getting me to bed.

I was wrong.

We didn't go to any school the next day.

We went to Brooks Brothers.

What a joint! Quiet, dull, almost holy, with a creepy elevator. Some of the clothes were not bad, a little wild in a queer sort of way. But I couldn't go near them. Suzy had this school catalogue, and she kept talking about a dark suit for Sunday Chapel. I thought maybe I could sneak in an Italian silk.

Instead, the salesman, who acted like he owned The

Drake, brought out a gray flannel suit. It felt like an army blanket. But that was it. They loved it. The queer little tailor kept measuring me--crotch to instep, crotch to instep--and Suzy paid extra to have it ready in an hour. It fit like a tank. They all kept patting me; you'll keep growing, ha ha ha, pinch on the bicep.

Man, I got out of there.

The only thing that saved me was one girl with enormous boobs who wrapped the package. She'd try to break the string and her chest would expand while she looked at me and then snap!, the string would break and she'd shake like jello as she smiled. Suzy didn't like her, but Suzy was jealous.

May I never have another day like that day! From the tailor to the barber where they shaved my head like it was a white sidewall, nothing left. Shoes I had to buy, no more alligators but heavy red ones, and white ones that made my feet look like balloons. Ties like prison shirts, shirts like button monopolies--buttons on the collar, the back of the collar, everywhere.

When they were done, Suzy was proud of me. I hated me. It wasn't me.

The next day we flew to New York. I had been in planes before, mostly private ones to Reno and Vegas. And compared to them, the big birds are dull. We went first class, of course, because Suzy had Mr. Loeb's credit cards. I was not impressed. The stewardess kept calling me Mr. Lieberman like she'd known me for years and I was about to be President. She was not so hot, but she looked better after a few martinis. Suzy was ordering them two at a time and the stewardess--Miss Harris--well, Miss Harris played it coy with a lot of "Are you old enough to drink?" and "Naughty boy" stuff.

About the third round I told her I was old enough to do anything she could think of. Miss Harris didn't know what to think of that for a minute, but Suzy ruined it all because she laughed.

Now Suzy's laugh is not exactly dainty. It comes out like a bowling ball and ends in a fit of coughing because she smokes so much. Mr. Loeb always asked her how a girl with such a beautiful chest could have such bad lungs. Did you ever think about that? When you see somebody really good-looking, ask yourself: I wonder what they'd look like if every other day they had to turn themselves inside out; you know, nostrils and lungs and colon all displayed.

Anyhow, Suzy's lungs are not the best from smoking and from years of hoofing it without much on, and she coughed and laughed and coughed, and I lost Miss Harris.

We checked into The Commodore in New York and Suzy started calling schools. We didn't waste time. We drove down to one that afternoon in a Mercedes convertible she rented.

What a joint it was! Like a country club it was, with tennis courts and football fields and ivy walls. It was August, but there were people all over the place. The football team was kicking around like it was the Chicago Bears' training camp. Suzy pulled up to a red brick building with ADMINISTRATION on it. There were two guys standing on the steps. Suzy showed a lot of leg getting out, and the guys almost dropped their pipes.

My sister has no sense of timing. Here we were in a school, and she walks past these jerks like she was on a runway at State and Lake-- mince, mince, little steps and lots of jiggles.

No, the Headmaster (that's what they call the cat) was not available.

Certainly we could make an appointment any time next week.

The secretary looked like she was scared of everything, especially me. I kept winking at her. She couldn't believe it, but she couldn't stop looking at me to see if I was winking.

Suzy tried to stamp on my foot.

It was just getting good--up with the eyes, wink, down with the eyes, blush, fluster--when this tall creep comes out of the office. He stared at Suzy like he was in the Salvation Army and he was there to save her.

Now once a guy looks at Suzy with grace abounding, she's won. And she milked this bit, let me tell you, with the tremolo voice and the teary eyes, all the time pulling her sweater tight across her boobs by pretending to look for a handkerchief in her purse, talking to him about how we couldn't come back next week, we just had to see him today.

He came in on cue. "Miss Quoon, I've told you before that my door is always open." Miss Quoon by this time hated all of us.

The interview--or should I call it Suzy's lament?--lasted for some time. I hardly said a word. I kept watching the guy behind his desk. He sat and swiveled in the afternoon sunlight. The sun came through the windows behind his desk. It served two purposes: it made a halo effect for his blond balding head, and it burned the eyeballs out of whoever was sitting and talking to him--sort of like the lights in the Hyde Park police station.

Suzy began by putting the check on his desk. The Headmaster looked at it from his chair.

I was filling out forms. Suzy was explaining how brilliant and advanced I was.

I was trying to write and listen. There was something

strange about this guy. Then it hit me: HE LICKED HIS WORDS! What a gimmick! Every few words and his tongue would flick out after the sounds, then lick his lips.

"Formal education (lick) is not, uh, everything (lick). After all, Aristotle said, 'Let early education be a sort of amusement' (lick)." He turned to me. "Don't you agree?"

"No sir." Teachers are like generals, my sister told me. You should always call them 'sir.' "I mean, I dig the idea. But Plato said it. *The Republic.*"

"Ah yes, that's right. Plato." (I thought he was going to lick, and I waited for it to come, but it didn't.) "You've read *The Republic?*"

"Yes sir. I'm taking an informal course in politics. From one of my sister's friends."

"A professor, I presume?"

"Yes sir. Of sorts." I couldn't figure this guy. "Anyway, I've read it."

"A distinguished book. The cornerstone of our political philosophy, don't you agree?"

"Not exactly." Here Suzy cleared her throat and shot a few daggers but it was too late. "Plato's got some creepy-crawly ideas about politics. You know, things like democracy giving equality to equals and unequals alike. Plato was a snob that way. Five to one if he was alive today he'd never listen to modern jazz, for example."

Man, I was in deep. Not a muscle moved. I could see the dust on his shoulders in the sunlight. I realized he never listened to jazz either.

"Your young brother is quite an original boy, Miss, uh, Lieberman. Of course it's late (lick) in the year to apply. Tests to take and all that."

They shoved me in a room and for four hours Miss Quoon

gave me I.Q. tests, achievement tests, all sorts of tests. I asked her for a blood test too, but that pissed her off.

Suzy waited in the car.

Being a Jew, I am aware of the polite brush-off, the extra smile, the false firm grip. Mind you, I am not neurotic about it, but I am ready for it. After the tests, as we said goodbye, I could smell it. Suzy swears I am wrong, that what happened next had no effect on my application. Me, I know better.

First, we got lost on the campus. It was easy to do. They had roads going in circles, roads into forests, roads around houses. It started to get embarrassing when we passed the same people three or four times. I wanted to ask directions, but Suzy was giggling and driving faster and faster. Pretty soon there was the Mercedes, a cloud of dust, and kids waving after us.

We passed football practice five times at least, and the whole team would wave and holler, and the Coach would blow his whistle.

The fifth time around the field and I made Suzy stop. I got out trying to cool it, like all I wanted to do was watch the practice.

Of course, Suzy had to follow me and make a big production of taking her heels off and walking in her bare feet, so by the time I got to the sidelines they were all watching her, and I was the only one watching practice.

Soon a big character comes off the field. He looks like an ape, heavy skin, big hands. He pretends not to notice us but he stops near us, guzzles water, spits it out, bites into an orange and spits the peel. The animal number; the watch-me-ain't-I-sweaty bit.

Suzy ignores him. I watch him.

Among other things, I figure I can make it in this school

if he's in it.

The Coach calls him: "Landowski, get ready to lead the laps." So he's the captain or something. So what?

He starts to talk to Suzy. She only smiles. Landowski's a wise guy. He's got a mammary complex and all the time he talks he looks right at her tits. He asks Suzy who the little boy is and can't she get rid of me.

I ask him if his name is really Landowski.

He looks surprised and says it is.

"Then," I say real quiet, "where's your harpsichord, Wanda?"

Suzy laughed. The ape turned white, then red. He didn't understand the insult. All he knew was I'd called him a girl's name. He screamed and came after me. I moved away. The team made a circle around us. I broke Landowski's jaw.

It was over very fast because you do not live in nightclubs all of your life and remain ignorant. I knew enough to take care of myself, what with expert tutoring by bouncers. I had to go for the jawbone because Landowski had all that padding on.

I was sorry. The Coach came over and almost cried. He chewed me out, telling me how this was their captain, this was a holder of a Yale Alumni Postgraduate Scholarship, this was--and he slowed down, looked at me carefully, and asked me why I hadn't tried out for the team.

"Because I'm not in this school."

"What are you doing here?"

"Trying to get into this school."

"Well, you've made a bad start, understand? I don't condone violence or dirty play. But, properly channeled, given the proper rein, aggressiveness can be a virtue." He was looking around, helping Landowski to his feet, motioning to his team to move away, which they did like a herd of cows. "You should apologize for your actions. I can't give you my highest recommendation, but, uh, but run over to the gym there and put on some pads and let's see what you can do, how brave you are in a sporting way."

What the hell, I thought, we're lost and can't get off the campus anyway.

Suzy sat down on the bench by the water buckets.

One thing before your heart begins to bleed for a poor youth brought up in nightclubs who has to go untried onto a football field--I knew more football than any of these jerks. Not that I'd played too much except at the Chicago Bears' training camp in Indiana where they'd let me go through light workouts, no contact, when Mr. Loeb flew us down. (He owned part of the team, I guess). Besides, the pro ball players got free booze at The Frolics, so I had my own teachers in the game.

It was not the easiest practice because I'd hurt their captain. The line didn't even block for me on the first play.

The second play I called, a roll-out pass, started the same way, but I remembered what Sid Luckman told me and I threw the ball as hard as I could into the linebacker's face.

They would have blocked for me after that but the Coach took me out, said I'd been dirty and ungentlemanly, and what was my name?

"Jerry Lieberman."

"Well, Lieberman, it is obvious that you have no understanding of this game. That was a filthy thing to do. You have now ruined two of my starting players. Do you know who that linebacker was? Do you know who you just hurt?"

"No."

"That was the son of the chairman of the board of

trustees!"

"He was red-dogging."

"Do you see the gymnasium, that huge building? The chairman gave us that. He gave us that, and he wants to see his son play. That may not be possible now, Lieberman. If you broke his son's nose, anything could happen. The chairman might even change his will. Just because of you."

"What should I have done?" (A little dialectic never hurt a coach.)

"Run!" (He said it real proudly, like a stripper in a police lineup for the first time.)

"Run? It was a pass play. I called a roll-out to the weak side and he blitzed on me."

"You should have run." (Now he had his nose in the air.)

"Look, it isn't logical. You had them in an umbrella with the ends floating. I had no guards pulling out. I had nothing, and with no linebackers left after the red-dog they were open in the middle and--"

"Lieberman, Lieberman. I am not a proud man. You are a big boy. You seem to know some football. Now, Lieberman, do you want to come here to school?"

"No. But I'm supposed to try."

"OK. If you come here, do you want to play football?"

"I don't care. Do I have to go to class?"

"Of course you have to go to class."

"No deals?"

"No deals. Certain advantages, of course, as any scholar-athlete deserves. But we are a preparatory school and there is no emphasis to speak of."

Now I am a hard dealer, a player of ice-poker, of cold chess, and the world to me is Machiavelli-made, good laws and good arms, power and property. But for a few special jerks I would do anything. Suzy being one such jerk, I told the Coach I'd play if he got me in the school.

Suzy was over by the water buckets, but she knew what I was doing, and she looked proud in her dumb way.

Now that I've been schnooked, canned, booted, I can look back on that joint as a circus. You know, a *clean* circus.

No more miserable life could I imagine. Why there was no revolution I could not understand--until I met some of the guys there and realized that this was what they wanted, that this school was some sort of guarantee for them, some order and contract with their society, with their parents and friends. But at first I did not know that.

I was put in Whitney House, run by Mr. and Mrs. Carp. Mr. Carp played the organ in chapel and walked on his toes. He was a little deaf, I think, because he played the organ so loudly our voices were drowned out. He was a good old jerk who spent most of his time in his garden, talking to his flowers. He was crazy and I liked him.

Mrs. Carp was very much younger with just a few gray hairs and with good legs, first-class Dietrich legs. In a place where there are no women, a chick like that can bother you and pull out all your complexes. She did not exactly make it easier, either, as she was not getting enough from him and it made her nervous. After every football game, when I got back to the house, she'd give me a big kiss. They got bigger from weekend to weekend.

Do not read tea and sympathy into this, as I deny everything.

Looking back, I realize that it was rough for them to keep me there through the season. Take the first day: I'm coming back from class. I get in the house and start to climb the stairs, not paying attention to what I'm doing, thinking about the creeps in their checkered vests and dirty white shoes. Those shoes threw me. I'm wearing white shoes, too, but they're really white, not all torn up, scuffed, beaten. I'm thinking how I'll never cut it here, how I try to wear the right things and I still walk in the wrong room.

OK, it's a stupid move, but the house is old and confusing.

What do I find? Three guys in suits, smoking and drinking martinis. At two in the afternoon.

So I stood there, and they looked at me like I was the Grand Inquisitor. Not a word. I figure they'll give me a drink. School rules, school schmools.

Finally a tall skinny bum gets up. He plays D.A.

"Aren't you a new boy?"

"Yeah."

"You should be in your room."

"Yeah."

"Look here, this may be against the rules, but it's a purely social thing. Now be a good boy and go to your room and don't say anything about this." (He had his arm around my shoulder by then and was pulling me out of the room.)

"My sister always says, 'If it's fair for one, it's fair for all.' I want a drink."

"Go to your room!"

"I'll go, but on my way I'll leave a little note for Carpy."

Silence. Ugly looks. I smile. He pours me a short one. I drink it.

"Now get out."

"One more for the road."

They come towards me. I back out. All the time they're calling me "New kike, new kike, Yid, Yid." I slam the door on them and catch a hand. I hear the scream and retreat to my room.

In those first few days I had broken several of their bones and this was not good.

Soon they stopped leaning on me, crowding me, and the treatment I got was like ice. No one spoke. No one nodded. I was nothing. I was not even there except for a few hours on Saturday, and even then the silence was terrible.

I would call signals and hear my voice coming back at me, and pad against pad would echo, the sock and sorrow of the game, knees cracking and shoulders wrenching.

For me there was no glory, and once when I scored both sides were silent, one from despair, the other from contempt. I remember the sun hitting my face.

I was so pissed I ran through the end zone and threw the ball into the pond. The refs went crazy trying to figure out a penalty for that one.

The last game of the season was the big one. The whole school went wild the week before the game. There were posters and rallies, and for a time it was kooky.

Friday night they had a bonfire in front of the gym.

The band was playing and they were throwing dummies dressed in Pelham School uniforms into the fire.

I was standing on the steps of the gym with the team.

For me it was uncomfortable watching the dummies fly-flopping into the flames, but none of the guys screaming and yelling were thinking what I was thinking.

An alumnus from the Class of '19 led the school in the cheer he'd composed as a senior:
>Poke Pelham
>Punch Pelham
>Poke poke poke
>When we're through with Pelham
>There'll be nothing left but smoke!

Everybody screamed this and the poor old alumnus got more and more excited, jumping up and down and spitting the words out through his bad bridge. The Headmaster finally came up and led him back to his seat.

The speeches by the team were ridiculous. There were roars from the crowd after each sentence. I could tell they were not listening, so I played with them as the bodies were tossed into the fire and the torches waved and the cheers went on.

"And now our quarterback, Jerry Lieberman!" (Moderate roar with some boos.)

"Thank you." (Bigger roar with more boos. A loose figure somersaults into the blaze. They're all frantic now, screaming, blind.) "Poke Pelham!" (That starts the cheering again.) "We're going to win." (Roar.) "Unt ve must vin mit der vootball!" (Roar.) "Ist das ist ein vootball?" (Roar.) "Ist you all gut little schnitzels?" (Roar.) "Sieg Heil!" (Roar.) "Sieg Heil!" (Roar.)

I cut it short because the Headmaster looked pissed. Given a little time to work on them, they might have burned the library.

The day of the game was a special day. No Saturday morning classes. No study halls. No obligations except Group Hate.

Cadillacs and Lincolns filled the parking lots and it was tweedy as hell: camel's hair coats, plaid skirts, lunches on the back doors of station wagons, Thermos bottles and flasks.

Since no one was visiting me, I sat in my room reading Burke. Dawn was still sending me book lists.

Like I said, I'm sitting there reading Burke when I hear these whistles and yells. They get louder. I think maybe the Pelham team has arrived so I go outside to take a look.

There, way across campus, some kind of movie star has arrived. There's a long limousine, and all the guys are crowding around a big blonde.

I laugh and start to go back to my room when I hear it: the voice of the bowling ball, the pickled vocal chords, setting the campus on its ear. "Jerrrreeeeeeeee!" it yells.

I look again and this blond is running across the grass towards me. In her heels and tight dress she looks like a cow on ice. And behind her comes this little fat guy who looks suspiciously like Mr. Loeb.

All this is being watched by the whole campus, whistling and jeering, and by Carpy, who has come out on the front porch.

"Jerreeee!" (Smooch, hug, love and sugar kiss.)

"Say there, kid, you're looking great. Have a cigar!" Mr. Loeb is very nervous and his eyes are glittering like footlights. He keeps looking at Carpy. The Carp just blinks and walks on his toes.

"No cigar, Mr. Loeb. I can't. It's against the rules." "Slip you one later on the sly, huh, kid?" Glitter glitter go his eyes.

"Jerry, we came to see the game. I got the weekend off. You like my wig, honey?"

Still the campus was shrieking and wailing and laughing. I wanted to get those two inside, but that meant steering them by Carpy. I had to introduce them.

The Carp was dancing across the porch. He was as uneasy as Mr. Loeb and he kept blinking like a rabbit.

I introduced them. Mr. Loeb decided to make a big show. "Hi there. How's this boy working out, huh? Pretty good, huh? Have a cigar. No, c'mon, have a cigar. Listen, I pay this kid's bills and I want you to have a cigar. That's better. Pretty good boy, huh? Listen, he's had a few troubles out here. You get him through, I'll see you get a little present, understand?"

Finally I got them through the door, leaving Carpy with his cigar.

Mr. Loeb was not impressed with my room. He gave me a lecture about the cost, about how it cost at least eighteen bucks a day, and for that you should have some style, some class: full-length mirrors, things like that. There was no arguing with him.

Suzy thought the room was quaint.

You read a lot about how the world is changed by small responses. You know, what if Luther had healthy bowels or Napoleon comfortable skin? Small responses make up our intelligence. Guts and teeth and adenoids all work on us.

Me, I am led by my nose, and with Suzy and Mr. Loeb in my small room I was happy for the first time in that room. I could smell the perfume and powder from backstage and Mr. Loeb's hair tonic and cigar smoke and blue-serge sweat, and it all came back, all the crazy confusion and independence.

Suddenly none of school made sense, none of the cheers or white shoes or social contracts. I wanted to be back with drums, breasts, smoke, liquor, light.

So let us make this short, let us cut it here. The chauffeur brought in lunch and drinks and I got drunk.

Training table training schmable. Give me sausages and fish and spices, all glubbed down with scotch, smoky scotch that I had not tasted for weeks. And cigars. And Suzy singing songs from *Pal Joey* and Mr. Loeb talking bigger and bigger, and me, eating and drinking and remembering.

When they finally broke in on us, I was skunked.

Landowski led me away.

They threw me into a cold shower but it didn't help much. They got me dressed. Somehow they kept me away from the Coach and they pretended to tape my ankles during warm-ups.

I knew then that they wanted that game. Because they protected me, they lied for me, and at the same time they hated me.

I kept asking myself: why should I get my ass busted? Why? Maybe everything would have been OK if Suzy had not made her grand entrance just after the kickoff. It was our first huddle and my head ached and I was trying to remember the plays.

There was this explosion in the bleachers and I could see a thousand horny bastards trying to look up and down Suzy's dress. She didn't help, either, bending over as she climbed into the seats.

That was it for me.

I called a bootleg and faked it gorgeously, so that when the lines piled up and the whistle blew, I was still holding the ball, standing near the sideline as if I was out of the play.

Then as they were untangling all the bodies, I walked over real slowly to the referee and handed him the ball.

Man, he was creamed. Immediately they tackled him. Both sides.

There was a silence all over while everyone tried to figure the situation.

It was time to cut out. The Coach was headed towards me, followed by the Headmaster, and behind him the students.

I started running around the gym, turned into the golf course and aimed for the tennis courts. One lap around the campus was all I knew I could make, but it might give Suzy and Mr. Loeb time to get back to the car.

I kept looking over my shoulder. The whole school was chasing me now, screaming, waving their fists, and I could see the Carp running lightly on his toes, surprisingly fast for a man his age, and the Headmaster, almost floating, like a blond angel, and Landowski pumping along, his face tortured by loyalty.

I couldn't get back to the parking lot. There were too many people after me, so I had to run out along the highway.

With luck the limousine would be along to pick me up. Without luck, they'd use me as the football the rest of the afternoon.

It was getting very close. I heard the car honking. I could hear Suzy cursing. The car was beside me. Landowski had just caught me by the shoulder and I couldn't shake him. I thought it was all over.

Suzy was calling him. "Landowski! Landowski!"

I wondered why she was calling him. I felt his hands let go. I dove through the half-open door of the limousine, past Suzy who was sitting there with the top of her dress down and her melons pointing towards an amazed, paralyzed group.

The car dug out and Suzy dressed up.

So those were the prep school adventures of Jerry Lieberman.

Now I am back in the free swinging life, not respectable, never dull.

Please do not think that I condemn those schools completely. After all, Burke said that he didn't know the method of drawing up an indictment against a whole people-- actually he said "an whole people," but that's a fruity way of talking these days.

"And," as I said to Dawn last night just before we started in on something that is none of your business, "if it's good enough for Edmund, it's good enough for me.''

Stream

Harold Holt

It makes no sense to have headphones when you've forgotten the cassette tape; all you find on the radio is static and depressing news: drive-bys, stick-ups, love murders, hate murders... Yeah, they're all crazy. How do I stand it? The music helps... So does the ride.

The Jeffery 6 is late, and the driver's rude; he doesn't even look at me as I slide my pass through the machine slot. He never looks at me. Sometimes I even speak, but I'm always ignored and forced to resume unacknowledged. I move toward the rear, and there's a fat woman in my seat, the seat I usually sit in. Now I have to sit on the right side with the sunrise against my jaw. Well, when I get to 71st Street, I'll just whip out something and pretend to read for a few blocks. That way, I won't have to see Carolyn's block, won't have to be reminded of that great year, year and five months, yeah.

Sometimes I'm like a hip-hop Dante passing through different levels of urbanized damnation via the CTA's finest. A rambler gets on at 79th; he would have been right at home on that bus, but he gets on mine. Don't really know what he's complaining about, but he curses a lot. Sitting right in front, he speaks to the air, the overhead posters, the windows, anything he figures will listen to him, like he already knows that most other passengers won't pay him any mind. He smells too. What's that odor? Mad Chi-town brimstone? The funk of spiritual failure? It's terrible; I've caught whiffs of homeless people that smell like roses compared to this. People cover their noses and open windows as the odor flows back, back, thick and oppressive.

I'm reminded of a woman rambler on the 79th Street bus I saw yesterday. She wasn't very old, but she looked as if she was. Her voice had been coarse and phlegmy during her male-bashing tirade. She had submitted that black men were all no good, and that her next marriage would be to an Arab or a "green man." If she knew some green men, I, for one, wanted to see that. The 95 East bus had a rambler also, a tall, spidery character who always wore a Bulls shirt and brown boots. He was always hyped up too, hollering about how he can't trust his cousins because they're always robbing him.

These early risers aren't as outspoken nor as engaging as the afternoon and evening reality performers. A man drew a gun one night on the Stony Island 28, a huge man who didn't really look like he needed a gun to back up his word. Maybe revealing the steel was a statement that pierced where his words only shouted. A couple of young women had their chains snatched on the 3 King Drive while an older woman had her purse snatched on the 4 Cottage Grove. On the 95 West, as the bus rounded a corner slowly, some teenage boys on the outside hurled an empty bottle through an open window, trying to hit another young man who'd just gotten on the bus. The bottle, miraculously, did not hit anybody; rather, it shattered against a pole, and the shards, also miraculously, did not injure anyone. However, the intent behind the careless action delivered a mental blow just as painful if not more so. On the 60 Blue Island bus, a Caucasian woman got on pointing in people's faces, quoting from the Good News Bible, the one written in contemporary speech, and she misinterpreted everything she read. According to her, the bible justified slavery and suicide, supported gambling and criticized leather, jewelry, Revlon products and WGCI's rap countdown. I'm not anything of a fashion prince, but even I knew that the outfit she wore was at least two years out of style. I figured her to be a hysteric victim of the recession, the one that only gentlemen and madams with heavy corporate investments are feeling directly.

People are reacting to the rambler now. There are still empty seats scattered about, so people move away from him. Of course, as the bus gets crowded, there isn't anywhere to go. Why are they so quick to avoid him? It's not like they're alien to some of the feelings and concepts he's expressing. What are they, afraid to see a darker shade of themselves? So sanctimonious with the prim and proper facades they sport daily? As sane and fit as I am, I respect a loon more than a liar.

I watch people ignore the rambler, ridicule him, mock him, slander him behind his back... That used to happen to me at work whenever I got fed up with the supervisor, coming down hard on any brother who wouldn't blow him or any sister who wouldn't pet him. Then that dip-head Peter, screwing up like that, making the rest of us look bad; then Gene the kiss-up, Flossie the Gossip and Brown the backstabber. I couldn't express myself around any of them, but I was spiteful and determined, right on up to my termination. Hell, my unemployment check is so laughable, I thought about faxing copies to Arsenio Hall and Joan Rivers for stage material.

The rambler's arguing now with someone sitting across from him. Why did they decide to speak out? Did they think they could stifle his miserable outbursts? Did they think they could scare him? All the passengers did was give the rambler a focus, a power base, a rod to bolt his message through. An irritated passenger spouts something about it being too early in the morning for the rambler's swearing. That's ridiculous!

Is it too early in the morning for one's heart to beat? Too early in the morning for that heart to feel, to rage? There's no allotted time for emotions! It's not like training a puppy to poop at a certain time!

More passengers start complaining, and the driver is urged to pull over. Now what? A call is made while passengers groan and complain. Eventually a police car pulls up and an officer gets on the bus. Of course his target is the rambler, and suddenly it's clear to me.

The rambler is taken off the bus by the officer so that the rest of these saints can resume their all-winning lives... One woman kisses the driver. He is the one with power, the one who makes or breaks the rebels he transports. The riders worship him like a shaman, he and his brood, the ones who allow the ramblers, the church ladies, the pickpockets and the chain snatchers to get where they need to go.

I've decided not to hit the job boards today, and my stomach kicks back twice. As I exit from the front, the driver's eyes catch me, and I linger there for seconds that are like minutes. He looks at me, fully, indepthly! He's never done it before, but he does it now. He smells the gin on my breath, and he knows me; he knows I understand.

A New Move

Arlene Greene

Joe woke with a start in the middle of the night, reached over for Aggie and found her side of the bed empty. He got up and tiptoed through the living room to the kitchen, making his way around the folding cot where Richard slept. Aggie sat at the kitchen table, picking at her fingernails and staring off at nothing like she was thinking real hard. Joe cleared his throat and felt afraid, although he didn't know of what. The knot in his stomach told him to turn around before she saw him and just go back to bed, yet the same knot drove him toward her.

"Aggie?" He almost continued "...what's wrong," but didn't. Aggie stared at the table in front of her for a long minute, sighed deeply and looked up at him. "You gotta go, Joe."

"Go where?"

"I don't know where...wherever you can, I guess. I don't know...we just can't make it like this anymore...I just can't make it like this anymore." Aggie spoke softly and deliberately, as if it were an effort to get the words out.

"What are you talkin' about? Aggie, come back to bed...you ain't making no sense." The knot in his stomach grew into a tight-fisted ball.

"You gotta go, Joe. It's the only thing I can think of. If you're not here, I can go down to the relief office. They'll give me money like they did before when you were gone, but they're not going to give me nothing if you're here." Getting this out seemed to revive her a bit.

Joe's fear flushed into anger.

"What?" He glared at her as the words sunk in. "Ain't this a hell of a fix...you're tellin' me to just go on off somewhere...kickin' me outta my own house...ain't I tried just about everything there is to try?" He paused, then shook his head in disgust. "I don't know what you people want from me."

He saw Aggie wince at the words "you people," knew she hated it when he lumped her in with the rest of the world, as if she were his enemy. But she let it go and went on. "Yeah Joe, you've tried everything, and that's just the point. There's nothing left for you to try...I gotta do something, and I don't know what else to do. The railroad ain't gonna call you back, Joe...it's in the paper all the time how they're goin' under...you can't keep expecting it to happen...it just ain't gonna."

Joe started to protest, to tell her how she was wrong about the railroad, but suddenly felt an overwhelming fatigue and sat down at the table across from her.

This fatigue, and the feeling of being drained that went along with it, was becoming too familiar. This lay-off had gone on longer than any other, and the energy it took to keep on hoping was getting hard to come by.

Aggie never worked but one day in her life, and so she couldn't be counted on to take over when Joe lost his job. She'd only gone to the eighth grade, had no job skills, and he knew the thought of being anywhere but home was frightening to her. Besides, Joe wouldn't have the faintest idea of how to take care of the house and the kids, he just wouldn't. Joe was the breadwinner and that was that, job or no.

Throughout the lean times, Aggie's skill was her ability to squeeze every last ounce out of whatever they had. She never let a bargain pass her by--put every crumb, bone, muscle and morsel of food to use, patched up and handed down clothing from biggest to smallest, saved and melted soap scraps and formed them into new bars, and kept spirits up by telling stories and making up games for the kids to play. It was difficult work, and sometimes Aggie's gift of "squeezing" wore hard on her. And these were the times the kids'd find her sitting still at the kitchen table, smoking her Pall Malls, drinking coffee, and not asking them lots of questions like she usually did.

Joe lit a cigarette and smoked it half way down before he spoke again. "Aggie?"

"What, Joe?"

Her tone of voice told him she didn't want to hear it, but he went on anyway.

"What if I went down to the precinct captain tomorrow? He said there might be a job coming up, and..."

Aggie cut him off. "Jesus, Joe...how many times has he said that? Besides, there ain't no election coming up. I thought about all that, and there just ain't nothing more you can do. Gettin' on relief makes sense, Joe. We'll still be together, just not every day...it ain't like I want you to go. It's just all there is left to do."

Sometimes, as a last resort, when there was absolutely nothing in the house and nothing to look forward to, Joe'd take to the streets, hit all the churches, ward offices, and charities in Englewood, and ask for food or money to tide them over. And Jesus Christ, he hated doing that. The pastor or precinct captain or social worker or whoever he had to see almost always seemed to think it their duty to give him an on-the-spot sermon or lecture along with the dole-out, and all it ever did was make him feel all that much worse for having to come asking in the first place. What made them think he'd be asking if he wasn't needing? They'd ask all kinds of questions, all the while shaking their heads and condemning him with looks that told him they either didn't believe him or thought him some lower type of life form.

"Seven children!" they'd say and cluck their tongues, or "No savings account?" as if everyone had one, and so he must be lying about it. He'd always tell them he didn't drink, even if they didn't ask. He was proud of this fact and wanted to make sure they at least got that straight. It never occurred to him that his saying this convinced them that drinking must surely be the cause of all his problems. Then, after the questions and answers, they'd start going on about responsibility and frugality and humility, as if any of that had anything to do with the fact that he was out of work, and that his kids were just plain hungry. He never said this, but sat and listened and hoped they'd get it over with and not go on forever. All he was listening for through these speeches was some indication that they were actually going to give him something. And sometimes he heard that they wanted something from him in return--a vote, or a promise to send his kids to their church, and he was always glad to hear this, because it meant he could say "yes" and they would give him something and he could leave. But sometimes it was hard to tell--sometimes they just went on and on and ended up telling him there was nothing they could do, and he'd think "after all that...."

The only exception was the Salvation Army. They never asked questions or gave advice or tried to make him feel bad. They'd just give because he asked, and for this he was grateful; but somehow it made him feel a little sick, and maybe as if he really didn't deserve to take what they offered.

He felt the need to explain, to tell them he didn't drink and that he tried hard to find work, but they never asked, and he'd leave the Salvation Army feeling heavy and low to the ground.

Going to the churches and charities was always a last resort, and easier to do if you knew the situation was only temporary, but this lay-off seemed different from the rest. Once a week, Joe'd take the 63rd Street bus to the yard at Stony Island and try to find out when he could get back to work. He heard the yard bosses talking about how the railroads were "under the gun" and how there was talk of cutting the work force--and how maybe those expecting to be called back might never be called back. He never told Aggie what he'd heard. He'd tell her things were "moving along," and "it wouldn't be no time at all he'd be back to work", and he tried not to notice the hard look she'd give him as she nodded her head and said "uh huh."

Now Aggie reached over and took hold of Joe's hand, gripping it firmly in her own. "It ain't your fault, Joe...it's just what is...maybe you can go stay with one of your brothers or maybe even Katherine or something..."

Joe yanked his hand out of hers and sat bolt upright in his chair. "I ain't asking my family for nothin'!"

Aggie's lips tightened into a hard line. "Dammit Joe...it's never mattered none that I've had to go begging to mine, has it? And over and over again, I might add. Gus and Maw never let me forget about the time they took me and Richard in and supported us while you were off Lord knows where for four full years...or how I've had to go to them time and time again for help." Her voice became hard. "It ain't like you ain't never left before!"

It was an old wound, and he could see she hadn't meant

to open it, for as soon as the words were out she reached back across the table to him.

Joe bristled anyway and pulled back farther, rejecting her touch. "Throwin' that in my face again...I told Gus I'd pay him back every red penny he put out on you back then and Goddamn if I won't...I don't need for you to be tellin' me who I owe...I know who I owe. And as for Maw...she ain't never had no use for me and you know it. I ain't askin' my family for nothin', and I told you not to ask Maw for nothin' either."

But Joe knew that sometimes Aggie had to go to ask her mother for help, that she hated to as much as he hated going to the charities, and that Sarah's sermons could put any minister to shame. He knew well what it was like for Aggie. Sarah would start off with "I know you're here for money again..." and then she'd go on about how she'd always known Joe was no good and how he'd never be able to provide for his family, and hadn't she always told Aggie she'd end up this way if she didn't listen to her, and on and on, and then she'd hand over some money. Sarah seemed to think that if only Aggie could see what a mistake she'd made, everything would be all right.

When Aggie returned from Sarah's, she'd throw her coat down on the chair, head straight for the kitchen with the groceries, slam them down on the table, and bang the pots and pans onto the burners. Every little thing the kids did or didn't do got on her nerves, and just looking at them seemed to remind her of Sarah's oft repeated "If you weren't so busy spittin' out all them babies one right after another, you wouldn't be in the fix you're in now." And so she'd yell at the kids more than usual and tell them to go away and just leave her alone. And the kids got used to it; whenever she came home from Sarah's house they tried as hard as they could to keep out of her way. And Joe would see her looking at him sitting there; and he knew she was beginning to believe all the things her mother said about him, that she felt just downright stupid for having made such an obviously bad choice in a husband. That look in her eyes made him feel ashamed and like he just wanted to go curl up in a corner somewhere and die.

Aggie took a deep breath and braced herself. She told herself she had to keep her train of thought. The point was Joe leaving, and not the old sore spot of "her family." She'd come to this decision through a lot of pain, and knew herself well enough to know she'd almost welcome an argument to sidetrack her, and allow her to become angry and not have to deal with what had to be done.

She changed the focus. "Joe, look. Marion's gettin' weaker, and I know she's going to be needing the hospital again. I can't take her to Cook County, I just can't. If I can get the relief, they'll take her in at Englewood, and I can walk there to visit her...you remember how long she was in the last time. I'm not talkin' forever, Joe. Maybe you can find something...I know you'll find something, but we gotta do something now until you do..."

Joe just sat there looking at Aggie, waiting for the answer to come to him, waiting for the words that would make this idea go away, words that would tell her everything was going to be all right, words he knew he didn't have in him. He put his head in his hands and squeezed his temples hard, then got up from the table without looking at Aggie and headed back to the bedroom.

Her tired voice followed him down the hall. "I'm planning on going down to the relief office day after tomorrow, Joe. There's nothing more to do."

Neither Joe nor Aggie slept that night, and while nothing more was discussed, Joe went out the next day and rented a room at 62nd and Union...two blocks from the house.

The following Monday morning, Joe sat looking out the second floor window of the rooming house. He'd flung the window open wide as soon as he woke up. The air in the room was stale and oppressive, and he'd thought he'd suffocate. Along with the cold air came the oniony odor from the White Castle across the street, and his stomach churned. There was someone in the hall grumbling and bumping around, most likely on their way to the communal bathroom, and the commotion reminded Joe that he had to buy a bottle of bleach for the bathtub. It was encrusted with brown and gray scum, and he knew it'd take a good half hour of scrubbing before he'd be able to set foot in it. He'd been taking "whore's baths" in the tiny sink in his room since he'd moved in last week, but he never felt clean. He felt a stirring in his groin at the thought of the bathtub and realized it was one of the few places he was able to be intimate with Aggie.

Sometimes, after dinner and a day of work or searching for work, Joe'd soak for a long time in a hot bath of epsom salts and think about what he was going to do for money the next day. If Aggie could pull herself away from the kids and the cleaning up, she'd come into the bathroom and sit on the edge of the tub and talk to Joe. Joe liked it when she did that--seemed like the only time they ever got together that was truly private. And they wouldn't talk about their problems at these times--Aggie'd reach over, grab the washrag, squeeze hot water over Joe's shoulders and ask him if it felt good. He'd close his eyes, knowing she didn't expect an answer. The bathroom was hot and steamy, and pretty soon Aggie's hair would start curling up around her face, and Joe'd look up at her, and then his eyes would travel down and trace the pearl of sweat that slid from her neck down between her breasts, and he'd reach out and cup them in his hands, and then Aggie'd close her eyes, and for a while she could tune out the sounds of the kids playing just outside the door and just listen to the sound of the water as Joe moved closer. If luck was with them, Aggie would slowly undress and end up in the tub with Joe, or else Joe would dry off and they'd lie down and wrap themselves in each other on a towel spread out on the floor. But more times than not, one of the kids would start banging on the door, whining about how he had to get in and "go pee," or the sound of the kids playing would suddenly change, and a scream that couldn't be ignored would pierce right through the warmth and the steam, and then quickly hands drew back and housedress zipped up; and, without a word to Joe, Aggie'd go flying out the door, and Joe would sink back into the tub and sullenly soak.

Joe shook his head to clear it, leaned out the window, and knew he'd better stop thinking and get going himself. But damn it all--right now it didn't matter how much sense it made or how logical it all was, her asking him to leave hurt, and it hurt bad. This was the first time leaving wasn't his idea. All Aggie'd ever wanted each time he'd left before was for him to come back. For the first time in his life Joe didn't feel like going to work. Felt like he could just sit hanging out that window all day without moving, and he did sit, for another half hour or so, until he saw the landlady, clutching her purse tightly under her arm, and remembered his weekly rent was due. The clock in the Barber Shop across the street read 7:10, and he cursed himself as he realized that all the daily pay jobs would be gone by now, but he got himself dressed and took off for Busch's on Wabash anyway. There might still be time to pick up a night shift dishwashing job in the Loop.

Joe got off the subway at Monroe, stopped off at Woolworth's on State for coffee, then cut over to Wabash and Adams to Busch's office.

Busch sat behind the desk shuffling papers and talking without looking up. "Got a good one for you today, Red--a live-in at Evanston Country Club in Skokie. Food, a room, and $40.00 a week--could go on the whole summer."

Joe hesitated. He'd taken on live-in jobs before, but always when he was hiding from Aggie and didn't want to go home. He wasn't hiding this time; this time she'd asked him to leave and that made it different, didn't it? He felt confused. He wanted to go home, but home to Aggie, not to the little room on 62nd Street. He couldn't think what to do--this time nothing he was doing was because he wanted to, and he couldn't think what he should do. He just didn't know what people wanted from him. Busch was looking at him quizzically, job ticket in hand.

"OK, what the hell? Sure, I'll give it a try." And he pulled out one of the four different social security cards he kept in his wallet. The name on this one was Joe Sexton--he'd gotten the name off the huge cans of vegetables in the restaurants he'd worked in. Busch never noticed the different names and numbers, or if he did he never mentioned it. As he filled out the job ticket, and signed it "Joe Sexton," Joe felt for the first time since he'd been forced to leave Aggie that he was back in control.

***

The knocking on the door was so sharp and abrupt that Aggie jumped, poking her finger with the needle. She lay the sock and darning egg down on the table and went to the door.
"Who is it?"
"Public Aid."
Aggie smoothed back her hair and wiped imaginary crumbs from the front of her Mickey apron and opened the door.
The caseworker was pretty. Young and petite and dressed in a tight blue suit. She carried a leather briefcase tucked tightly up under her arm and walked into the room as if she'd been expected. Aggie smiled nervously, but the caseworker did not return her smile. Moving through the room and looking around to each side as she spoke, she identified herself, "I'm Miss Shaw, I'm here for the home visit. I have some questions to ask you and some forms to fill out."
Aggie, still standing by the open door, closed it, feeling vaguely as though she should apologize for something, although she certainly wasn't quite sure what it could be. She followed behind Miss Shaw as the woman headed through the living room into the kitchen.
"How many people live here?" Miss Shaw threw the question behind her without turning around. She was bent over her briefcase, and when Aggie didn't answer right away, she looked up at her.
Aggie felt flustered and answered, "Six...no five really, although Johnnie may be back soon." Miss Shaw raised her eyebrows and looked Aggie in the eye.
"You don't know how many people live here?"
"Yes, I do...I mean, well, Marion's in the hospital, but she lives here, and Johnnie's gone off, but he'll be back, and then there's Margret..."

They'd reached the table, and, without looking at Aggie, Miss Shaw pulled out a chair, sat down, began shuffling through her briefcase and said, "Sit down, Mrs. Sawyer."

Aggie obeyed the command, and sat on the other side of the table, fingering the rickrack on the neck of her dress.

Miss Shaw pushed a stack of papers across the table with instructions to "Sign everywhere I've made an 'X,'" and Aggie complied.

"Now, I need to know what you've been doing for money since your husband left."

"Well, I don't have any money."

"But you must be eating."

"Well, I've just about gone through all the food we had, and that's why I applied for welfare, 'cause I don't know what I'm going to do."

Miss Shaw took notes as Aggie spoke.

"You applied for 'Emergency Benefits,' and I have to check your cupboards and closets to determine need." She did not meet Aggie's eyes and was already up and out of the chair.

Aggie jumped up and opened the tall metal cabinet where she stored the staples and canned goods. There was a bag of flour, a can of tomatoes, spices, and a bag of macaroni shells. Miss Shaw again took notes and moved to the refrigerator. Inside was a carton of milk (Aggie'd mixed up some powdered), a half-empty package of lard, and some withered vegetables.

"Looks like you could make some biscuits and spaghetti here! I have to tell you that Emergency Benefits are for just that...emergencies."

"But they told me it might be two or three weeks before I got a check."

"Yes, that's right. There's a process that must be..." "But even if I make spaghetti, the kids'll eat it up and it'll be gone in two days...that's why it's an emergency," Aggie explained.

"You could reapply, you know."

"But they said it takes three weeks to even get emergency benefits."

"Yes, that's right." Miss Shaw seemed pleased Aggie finally understood.

Aggie started to say something, but Miss Shaw was already on her way down the hall. She stopped in front of a doorway. "What's this room?"

"That's where the boys sleep."

Miss Shaw pushed aside the flowered curtain covering the door and poked her head inside.

"Who's that?" she asked, pointing over to one bed where a shock of brown hair stuck up from out of the covers.

"That's Robert, he's thirteen."

"Why isn't he in school?"

Aggie didn't answer right away, but waited until Miss Shaw pulled her head back into the kitchen.

"Robert's retarded. He stays home with me."

This was important enough to write down, but Miss Shaw did not comment. They went on through the living room where Aggie explained the sleeping arrangements, Sharon on the couch and Richard and Joe Jr. on the foldaway cot, then went through to Aggie's room. Miss Shaw pulled open every drawer of Aggie's dresser and made notes on the contents. Nothing here to worry about. Most of Aggie's clothes came from Goodwill, except underwear, and when Miss Shaw opened that drawer Aggie wanted to run and hide. There was no way to hide all the holes in her panties, no matter which way they were folded. After the tour was over, Aggie walked with Miss Shaw to the front door.

"I have what I need and will go over the case with my supervisor. Now that we have your husband's social security number, we'll attempt to find him, and we'll be contacting your relatives to determine their ability to help out. You'll be advised of your eligibility when we've completed the process." Aggie closed the door and was consumed with thoughts on what she had to do now to insure getting the check. She hoped Joe'd had enough sense to use another social security number, but she couldn't be sure and would have to check on it. She'd also have to visit her mother and Gus to warn them about what she knew they'd consider an intrusion on their privacy, not to mention one more indication of what a louse Joe was for forcing his family to go on relief. She'd have to get a note from the hospital about Marion, and rent receipts from Mr. Cohen and send them off right away. She almost felt happy. These were things she could do; these were things to think about and to do, and that would make things better.

Aggie went into the boys' room and shook Robert awake. "C'mon, you gotta go over and get Maw to come and stay here for when the girls come home for lunch. I gotta go out for a while."

She was already untying her Mickey apron and heading for the bedroom, as Robert was lifting himself up and trying to understand what she wanted.

"Where you goin', Momma?"

Aggie thought for a minute, then yelled out, "To the store."

***

Aggie walked over to 62nd Street, checking the address on the slip of paper in her hand against those on the buildings.

Exceptional, for February

Michael Fitzgerald

It was almost noon before the girl stirred, though a hangover and some monster congestion had been hammering her head for hours. The twin ills dulled the shock of waking up some place she'd never seen before to hear a knowing stranger say 'good morning.' Even though she looked like she'd had a terrible night, she was still sexy as hell, and Patrick felt his loins stir.

"I thought he was going to kill you," said the girl, in a voice croaking with sleep and alcohol.

"Who?" asked Patrick, loins suddenly still.

"Robert, the really dark guy at my table."

"Oh," said Patrick, relieved it was no one he knew. In the pause that followed he could almost hear happy alcohol molecules singing in her brain. "Why would he want to kill me?"

"You were leaning all over our table, talking that racial stuff, and he was getting madder and madder, and I was sure he was going to jump up and start beating on you."

Patrick was puzzled by the thought of someone having wanted to hurt him, especially last night. He'd been so friendly, and one of the guys at her table had bought him a 7&7. He was light-skinned, though, so it must've been the guy on the other side of the table, the one the girl -- did he know her name? -- was next to.

He had met the girl at the Tiki, on his way from the bathroom to the window booths his friends jammed. He had been walking carefully, so as not to alarm his body into something dramatic like projectile vomiting, when some guy at a booth had called out to him.

"My man, what up?"

And Patrick had stopped, turned and said "You, baby, you."

"No, really, what's happening there, with all these people?"

It was, after all, Tuesday night at the Tiki, usually a quiet time.

"It's my birthday, so I'm trying to get as drunk as possible, and my friends are helping me," Patrick had said.

The guy had laughed then, and said, "Oh yeah? How old are you? And why you want to get drunk? You can do that any night."

"I'm 25, and getting drunk is an experiment. You see, people reveal their true selves when they're drunk, and I want to see what that is for me."

The guy laughed again, and said, "What's your name?"

"Patrick. What's yours?"

The guy had told him, and introduced him around the table.

Though well on his way to a lopsided victory over sobriety, Patrick noted the booth's five black inhabitants, three women and two men, were barely old enough to drink. Two of the women looked like sisters, the other looked too good to be related, it seemed to him. He figured two of them were out with their boyfriends, and the one's sister was tagging along. Patrick remembered none of their names now.

"Well, why are you here?" Patrick had demanded.

"Just hanging out, having a few."

"That's cool, and it's cool that you come to the Tiki to do it," Patrick said. "That's what I like about the Tiki--not only can you get ice cream here until four in the morning, but it's integrated. I think more places should be integrated--too many black people and white people don't know anything about each other in this town, you know what I mean?"

"I hear you," Patrick was sure the guy had said.

"I mean, too many whites think black people can't speak properly, and too many blacks think white people can't dance. And it seems like a lot of people of both races hate the other for no reason, just because they've never spent time together. This bar is good for the future of America!"

Patrick was pretty sure the guy had laughed, and remembered him calling the waitress and saying, "Get this man a drink--what're you drinking? A 7&7? Get him one of those, on me!" Then Patrick had carefully staggered back to his table.

He even thought he'd been back to the girl's table, for more friendly conversation, at some point after he'd revealed his true self to be a happy, roaring drunk. He vaguely remembered saying something at some point about how white people secretly admired blacks as having more soul, as being outside society and freer for it, able to disregard the normal inhibitions of the white world. But maybe he had just thought that. In any case, he was glad Robert hadn't hit him. Besides, he didn't think he had said anything offensive.

"Why was he mad? What was I saying that would make him mad?" Patrick asked the girl.

She shook her head once, gently, the way a grandfather clock's pendulum counts time, as if she didn't want to be awake enough to explain social nuances to some clearly ignorant white male.

She herself was half black and half white, with cafe au lait eyes, a smile like dawn sun and a figure that must've been drawn.

How had she come to be here in his dust-filled, wretched little room? How had he managed to get her into bed, and more importantly, how was he going to rouse her from her obvious tiredness to do it again?

Her voice cut through his plotting. "It's just not a good idea to tell black people they really have it good compared to whites. Even when we do well, whites think it's only because we got a break from the government, and blacks think you must be an Uncle Tom."

Patrick remembered a black professor at the University of Chicago he had interviewed once, who had talked about the frustrating paradox of affirmative action, and the damage it had done to blacks, as people forgot it existed to right a wrong, and instead looked at it as a wrong in its own right. He didn't know how to respond to this, and was spared when she spoke again. "Where's Tanela?" asked the girl -- what was her name? Oh yes, Breeze, a perfect fit, he thought -- untamed yet gentle.

Tanela had been a problem. Built-in security for Breeze, supposed to protect her from Patrick. The three of them had left the Tiki together, walked to Patrick's massive Hyde Park apartment and began drinking wine. Tanela seemed very alert, Breeze seemed almost asleep, and Pat had figured all was lost.

Come to think of it, he usually thought all was lost just before he ended up in bed with someone.

Which is what happened, as Tanela drank herself unconscious, and he and Breeze headed for his bedroom. Much later, he had gone back to carry a snoring Tanela into his room, to prevent his roommates from an unpleasant surprise and himself from an unpleasant argument.

"She had to go. She said to tell you she'd call you later."

He was looking at Breeze, feeling a little sorry for her -- she did not look enthused about life. But he was mostly looking for some sign that she might be interested in a little replay of last night. Earlier that day, actually -- they hadn't staggered out of the Tiki until 3 a.m. The Tiki, had to be the least likely bar in the world for a pick-up. Any place with ceiling lights shaped like enraged blowfish was not going to inspire happy trysts, as a rule.

She made a face. "Stop staring."

"I can't help it," said Patrick, who almost told her she was the most incredible woman he'd ever seen. This wasn't quite true, but certainly very close to the truth. Besides, the more he looked, the more frustrated he got that they had both been too drunk to come. This should be remedied. The whole experience was obviously missing a climax, and as far as Patrick was concerned much less satisfying. She seemed uninterested in satisfaction.

"Would you like some water, or some orange juice?" Patrick asked, hoping perhaps this might stimulate her.

"Do you have any coffee?"

Patrick hesitated. He himself did not drink coffee, but two of his roommates did. Coffee was certainly more stimulating than orange juice, or so he'd been told. Personally, caffeine worked on him much like his biology text had said it would -- not at all, unless he got excited by something. He made a decision.

"Yeah. Let me get some for you." And he walked out into the kitchen, and went rummaging through the better of the apartment's two refrigerators, which coincidentally was used by his coffee- drinking roommates.

***

"So, did you make it home all right the other night? I

know those late-night walks can be dangerous, especially when you don't know your companions."

The leer on the other end of the phone was Cedrick's. He had been at the bar until the prurient end. Cedrick actually outdrank Patrick that night. This was difficult to imagine, since Patrick had violated the Tiki covenant of "thou shalt drink only one Zombie," swallowing three during a game of hide-the drink played against a vastly outnumbered waitress. The three Zombies equalled 21 shots of rum by themselves, let alone all the other drinks he'd consumed. It was a good night for breaking covenants: Patrick later figured out he had violated seven of the Ten Commandments.

"Yeah, I was fine, by then," Patrick said, a bit expectantly. Cedrick was not one to avoid an opportunity for a dig, especially at a straight friend.

"You should've been with your little friend there. You were all over her."

Patrick did not remember this. In fact, he didn't remember much of what happened between 1 and 3. He didn't even remember how Breeze had ended up at his table.

"I was?"

"Oh, you were like a remora on a shark. I thought we were going to have to put a screen around you, or maybe the bar owner would come over with a crowbar to separate you."

"Noooo. I don't remember that," Patrick said, his voice pitching higher, as it always did when he was embarrassed.

"It's true."

This explained why sweet-faced, foul-tempered Colleen, the first good-looking waitress within memory to work at the Tiki, was so cold to him now. Patrick had, he vaguely remembered, finally convinced her that he was not just some typical male asshole -- yes, that's how she put it that night

-- and she had said she would have a drink with him when her shift was over, to celebrate his birthday. He suspected, though he couldn't be sure, that this had not happened. A blown opportunity.

"So what happened?" asked Cedrick.
"Well, I uh brought them back here."
"And?"
"And we ended up in bed."
"Both of them? That's very good. I'm impressed."
"Don't be. Anyway, she's the only one that matters."
"Will you see her again?"
"I'm sure of it."

***

Patrick popped questions at her while he attempted to make coffee. He learned she was 17, (which meant he had broken Art's Law, Art being a friend of his who said you should never sleep with anyone less than three-quarters your age), a freshman at Columbia College but not doing much studying, though she liked it better than the high school she left out of boredom. Her parents had a situation-normal relationship and so were now divorced.

She lived with her mom in the bad part of Kenwood, near 43rd and Kimbark.

This wasn't world-class ghetto, like some parts of Chicago, but it made his area look like Astor Street. His building, a patrician Hyde Park six-flat when it was built in the 1920s, was now one of the worst, and it wasn't bad. Like most of these reminders of an age where opulence came cheap, it was a student ghetto now, with at least five people living in each apartment save one, occupied by an eccentric former student who enjoyed baiting Tomas, their Eastern European landlord.

Patrick brought her some coffee. She drank it black. They were sitting on the futon that ruled the space between the assorted papers, books and dustballs that made up the kingdom of his room, which in grander days belonged to the servant. She sat against the wall, leaning against it with her knees drawn up as if to prevent her from sliding off it. He sat at the other end of the bed, cross-legged.

She showed him a picture of her father, whom she seemed to like more than her mother. The picture showed a scruffy Jewish man with a drinking problem.

"You must get your looks from your mother," commented Patrick.

Breeze frowned a bit, and put the picture away. Patrick, part curiosity and part wanting to shift the topic, tried to be playful as he asked, "Do you often wake up places you've never seen before?"

"This isn't the first time," she said. "I've had a lot of guys."

"All races and creeds and religions?"

"You're not the first white guy I've slept with, no, and you won't be the last."

Patrick was tempted to say he'd be the best, but thought better of it.

"Are you one of those white guys who has some kind of fantasy about sleeping with a black woman?"

"No, I was just teasing. You're the one who said you'd had lots of guys."

"I have. I don't like sex that much, though." For some reason, her tone of voice reminded Patrick of a woman he knew who'd been molested. His goal was slipping away, so he changed the subject.

"Do you have a job, or do you just go to school full-time?"

"No, I don't have a job. I need to get one, because I don't have enough money to pay for school without it. But it's hard to get a job without a high school diploma. It seems like any job I could get would bore me, but if it sounds interesting, I don't qualify."

"What about secretarial jobs?" asked Patrick.

"I can't type," she said.

"Oh, that would be a problem, then," Patrick acknowledged, dumfounded that people in the modern age could not know how to type.

"Well, here's what you do: get the boss alone, and you talk to him a bit, and tell him about your willingness and desire to learn, and be earnest and be sure the door's shut and you're dressed sexy, and he'll give you a job, I'm sure."

Breeze did not respond.

Patrick had worked himself close to her during this flight of fancy, and said, "You are incredibly attractive, you know."

He kissed her, and kissed her again, and she responded for a moment, then turned away slightly, her tone mischievous and pleased, her words not: "Stop that!"

"Why?" he asked, kissing her again.

"Because I like it, and I'm not in the mood." He smiled then, and backed away a bit.

"I was thinking of modeling, actually," she said.

"Well, you're gorgeous, and you have a great body, but you're probably too short," offered Patrick.

"I have a friend who's a photographer, and he says he'll help me put together a portfolio," said Breeze.

"Yeah, well, be careful -- I would never trust a guy with a camera."

Patrick suspected the photographer wanted to take pictures of her naked, as a thin pretense to getting her into bed. He shook himself. Jealousy, already? All men were not like him.

"Give me a break -- he's my friend," said Breeze, reading Patrick as if he were a billboard. Then she laughed.

***

"Schheheheheh," came the half-laugh, half-spit voice over the phone. "You're something else, you know that?"

"What?" challenged Patrick, voice rising. Stu couldn't know. Stu couldn't be allowed to know. Stu would bring this up again and again, embellishing it each time until it had a sort of rococo texture to it, and even Patrick would find it interesting to hear. Patrick would hate most that it would remind him of one fluke success with a gorgeous woman.

"You were so drunk, it was coming out yer ears; I couldn't believe it."

Stu couldn't believe most things he believed. Patrick thought this made him a sort of self-atheist.

"Scheheheh. So what about the one?"

Patrick suspected Stu knew something. His eyes rolled, involuntarily. Thank goodness the phone would keep Stu from seeing.

"What one?" Patrick asked, hoping it was just another case of Stu having a crush on someone Patrick knew.

"You know, that cute little black girl you were all over. Scheeheheheh."

"What about her?" Patrick said, as innocently as possible.

"Oh come on, you can't fool me. You wouldn't miss an opportunity like that in a million years. You went home and pinga-pingaed, and you know it." The probing, righteous

Stu then slipped into a slyer tone of voice.

"Are you gonna see her again?"

"I don't know," Patrick said, thinking that he'd surely like to.

***

She was almost done with her coffee, and did seem perkier. Not that this meant much.

"What time is it?" she asked.

Patrick scrambled to find his clock, buried under something he'd been reading.

"It's 12:50," he reported.

"Listen, I've got to go. I'm supposed to meet someone for lunch," she said.

"Hey, it's kind of chilly out. Do you want to borrow a sweatshirt or something?"

Actually, it was warm, exceptional for February, and she could get by without the sweatshirt, but he felt it might bring them together again.

"Um, okay," she said, a little reluctantly.

Pat went to the closet and rummaged through his Elfa shelves. He wouldn't give her his U of C sweatshirt -- too grubby, and UC charged too much for them if he didn't get it back. The blue sweatshirt didn't really mean anything, but it cost $50, and was probably too heavy.

He found a light sweatshirt he had received on his first assignment for the Sun-Times, a souvenir from a youth camp that focused on battling drugs and peer pressure. He was inclined not to lend it to her, because it did mean something to him, but he wanted to give her something, and it was the right weight for the day. He also hoped somehow she would understand it meant something to him, so she would have to see him again.

"So, let's have lunch some day, okay?" Breeze said as she gave him her phone number.

"I'd like that," said Patrick, suddenly confident he would sleep with her again.

At the door, they kissed goodbye with some feeling, and he stood on the sun porch and watched her walk away.

He never saw the sweatshirt again.

The Dog on the Porch

Timothy Willis

The dirty black terrier atop the porch barked and barked angrily, and would not permit Alvin Mathers to pass the rusty iron gate and climb the stairs to press the doorbell. He stood there, just behind the gate, looking at it; and it, bouncing up off its thin front legs and tiny, round paws with each shrill bark, looked back at him.

"I wonder what he's trying to tell you," called a neighbor, who walked through the screen of the house just next door.

Alvin glanced over to her and smiled, half-embarrassed. "Well, if it's 'I welcome you and embrace you, good friend' I think the delivery is being illustrated improperly."

On Alvin's "Well" all through "improperly" the small dog cried, growled and stamped about the porch even more furiously.

"They named him Claudius."

"Oh yeah?"

"After the guy in *Hamlet*."

Alvin grunted in affirmation.

"That's Shakespeare, y'know."

"Yes, I know."

"They had called him--well, Mrs. Jennings had called him--Ebony, y'know, because of his color. But when still a puppy he killed the only other surviving puppy of a litter of five. Then Sam called him Claudius. A lot of people around here just call him Cloud or Black Cloud or 'that damn dog.'"

Alvin politely listened, although he was quite agitated by

the entire predicament. "You said, 'Sam,'" he interpolated brusquely. "You mean Samantha Jennings?"

"Oh, yeah. Her brother is Samuel but everybody calls him by his nickname: Nip. Behind his back he's mostly called 'that good for nothing son of a bitch.'"

"As loud as the dog is, shouldn't Samantha, or someone, have checked the commotion by now?"

"I did," the neighbor said simply.

"No, ah, I mean, from here."

"Usually when the dog's out like that it means nobody's home."

Alvin raised his hand over his eyes to ease the glare of the sun, which hovered just behind the even row of dilapidated Cape Cod houses, and to have a better look at the neighbor. The landscape of Eighty-fifth and Wallace Street was like an architect's ancient blueprint--once crumpled tightly and discarded into a puddle, then retrieved and unfolded. The shade offered by his hand was not much of a difference; all he could make out of the neighbor was a brilliant orange silhouette that was in a definite feminine shape; but whether she was comely or otherwise, he could not discern.

"I'm expected, though," he said to her.

The neighbor swayed back and forth on her heels with arms akimbo. "You're expected to do what?"

"What I mean is, I just talked to Samantha an hour ago; she knew I was coming." Staring for clarity of vision, his countenance took on an agonizing expression. Yet, but from her stance, he could not even distinguish the colors of her clothes, or where one article began and ended with another.

"You sure she wanted to see you?"

The dog, which had begun growling low and barking with less enthusiasm, as its attention was wrested away from Alvin to other things shifting in the cool September breeze, began again, energetically, without the hoarseness it had begun to display.

Alvin grimaced at the dog, then again addressed the neighbor: "Would you mind if I used your phone to call here?"

Alvin watched the silhouette, which was motionless. He thought he heard a harsh exhalation, which might have indicated displeasure at his proposal, but it could also have been a breeze. There did, however, issue forth annoying sucking sounds from her mouth as she mulled her decision over.

"I'd only be a minute," he continued, hearing a slightly perceptible desperation in his own voice. He stood away from the gate, stood straight, smiled with affable exaggeration, and opened his sportjacket. "I look safe enough, don't I?" Inwardly, he surmised her thoughts that it was he who may have been in jeopardy, who was out of his element, far, far from his comfortable and well-kept apartment in Printer's Row. He released the jacket and, with his arms still out, he spun with the finesse of a runway model, revealing his white polo top beneath the blue wool jacket, the Edwin jeans, and the black leather, brown trim driving shoes. "How 'bout it?"

"After a show like that--why not?"

Alvin hurried across the cracked pavement, past the unmown lawn overrun with dandelions, up the neighbor's porch, and was ushered in. He stopped just within the door, but was inadvertently bumped on in as the neighbor entered and closed the doors behind her.

"What's your name anyway?" she asked, directing him into the living room.

"Oh! Alvin. Alvin Mathers. And yours?"

"Kim--berly Connors. Friends call me K.C. You can call me Kim."

"Oh, *haha*," chuckled Alvin nervously and genuflectively.

"I have to get the phone," she said rather awkwardly, suddenly bashfully. "You have a seat."

She walked away, then stopped and turned as she reached the threshold that separated into another room. It was then that Alvin took a complete survey of the neighbor. At first sight one would think her older than the teenager she must have been, for she was tall and leggy (in a pair of worn, fitted shorts), shapely and svelte (as outlined in a dingy white t-shirt), and unexceptionally pretty. Her face was dark, her eyes wide, her expression youthfully simple, yet also it revealed an educated past, whether through textbooks or experience. From her environment she had acquired a saucy tone, Alvin theorized, but the intent was genuinely sweet.

"Uh," she started, then appeared to have forgotten her thought or was considering how to phrase it. "Do you want something to drink at all?"

"No," said Alvin, and almost blushed for her, as if she were suddenly aware of his examination of her; and almost for himself, for having examined her then looking her directly in the eye. "No, thank you." "Is something wrong?"

"No, no. Nothing."

She smiled mildly to his embarrassed smile and disappeared. Alvin remained standing. The room was small and dusky. The oversized sofa and armchair were both covered in plastic. The coffee table was clean, dusted, and atop it were clashing ashtrays at either end, and an open candy bowl in the center filled with wrapped peppermints. The walls were white and bare, but for one painting on the far wall. On black velvet canvas was a sketch of a black terrier outlined in soft blue, facing ahead in a sitting position with its head cocked to the left.

In the house, somewhere, a re-mix of some Motown classic was turned on and lightly showered the silence. Alvin could not tell from where it emanated, for it seemed to just rise into the air from nowhere and from everywhere, and Alvin could not imagine the house having ever been still and funereal. He hummed along and stared past the gaudy lamp that had been set beside the armchair on a round table, which was similar to the coffee table, and out the window until the young neighbor returned.

"Here. Cellular."

He took the cellular device, frowned at the grit around it, but placed it over his ear nevertheless as he felt the neighbor's wide eyes on him. He checked for the dialtone, then dialed. "It's awfully quiet," he said, glancing over to her as he pressed the digits smoothly and rapidly. "You're the only one here, huh?"

"Why?" she asked blankly, rocking again on her heels.

"No reason, I just--Hello, hi, Samantha? It's Al. I'm at your neighbor's--Kim Connors, right next door. Look, I tried"

Alvin's eyes shifted involuntarily from side to side, as he went mute. His lips hung ajar. He stood still, the lids of his eyes narrowing and widening in search of comprehension. "But."

He glanced around the room, finally setting his careless, wandering gaze on the neighbor. His expression was one of bewilderment. "What are you talking about? You *invited* me--uh huh, yeah..."

Alvin's vision followed as the neighbor cast her eyes down to her bared feet, which were not at all as unattractive as feet could possibly be. The large toes were not so large, and the smallest ones had cute slices of nail across them. The nails on all were trim and polished in a shiny pale pink. One foot rubbed smoothly against the other. "I-I don't understand you at all," said Alvin, suddenly flushed and aggrieved. "I came all the way-"

Alvin and the neighbor made unintentional eye contact, and he turned his back on her, for her expression was too irritatingly ingenuous, too simple, too full of innocent satisfaction with everything. "Look, I am over at your neighbor's house, okay?" he began to whisper into the receiver. His teeth clenched. "Just let me not be a burden on her and let me come over so we can discuss this. Okay? Okay?"

A second passed and Alvin swore beneath his breath, and could not suppress an agitation that produced angry tremors through his body. He began to pace, became conscious of it, flashed another glance towards the neighbor, who had again vanished, and gave in to the habit. He walked stiffly the length of the coffee table then back, then repeated the action. "What? What? Your brother what? Wants to use the phone?"

The neighbor padded softly into the room after several minutes had transpired with a glass in her hand. Alvin sat in the armchair, one hand stroking his moustache absentmindedly, the other caressing the phone that laid on the round table.

"Orange juice?"

He took the glass. "Tastes good, despite the absence of vodka." He smiled weakly.

"Did you want some?" she replied almost meekly, just standing over him.

"No," he said unimpassionately. "I was joking. I heard it somewhere."

"Are you going over?" she asked in a faraway voice.

"I did threaten to barge over there, kill the dog if it crossed me and enter, but she was babbling something about her brother using the phone and I don't think she heard me or just didn't think much of my threat." He cleared his throat. "Y'know," he said plaintively, examining the Snoopy and Woodstock characters on the glass, "I took off work with no valid explanation, no nothing. I said I'd explain later. And, I really don't know what I was charging over here for, myself."

"Where do you work?"

He stared deeply into Snoopy's collar, his vision going blurry, his thoughts returning to the little LaSalle Street advertising agency. He then looked up at his hostess in a state of alarm and began to rise.

"I'm sorry. I'm just rambling and all. I've imposed too long. You must've had homework or chores to do...." "It's all right."

"Well, I'd better go," he said after a pause, thinking by her tone that her statement was not yet done. "Thank you very much for the OJ and the use of the phone."

"Are you going over there?"

"No, I think I've wasted enough time on that one, don't you agree? That's what I get for meeting girls at city colleges," he said as an afterthought, though inaudibly.

"Yeah, she's nuts," the neighbor answered the first part, staring through the window; and as Alvin grunted, she continued in a serious tone: "All of them are nuts. The dog's the sanest thing. It just doesn't like anybody just because it doesn't. Reasons aren't really necessary. When there is a reason, somewhere in the back of it, on the side, something is not right, not complete, not--" She struggled.

"Valid?"

"Yeah, valid. Valid. And, anyway, there's a reason *for* one thing and a reason *against* the same thing. And to look at both sides evenly, with nothing to gain or lose, they both sound good, make sense--and *that* doesn't make sense, does it? But the dog just doesn't like people, any people, and he has no reasons why, and he barks and hates happily."

"What grade are you starting?" asked Alvin, both tired and nonplused, as he stepped outside.

"Ninth," she said proudly, suddenly springing out of her meditative voice. "Freshie power. Class of '94." She smiled shyly, yet brightly.

Down the porch and across the ragged street unlocking his car, Alvin attempted, something else at the neighbor, as she slid against the railing and picked at the peeling paint, but the terrier leapt up on its porch and bounced up and down, snarling, barking and growling at him and the echoes rose all over the quiet neighborhood.

A Plundered World

Hoyt Fuller

Carl packed the toilet kit in the two-suiter and looked about the room to see if he had forgotten anything. Except for an ashtray with several cigarette butts in it on the top of the dresser, the room was as he had found it when he arrived two days before. It was his old room, the one he had occupied as a child, and the one he always used on visits to his grandmother. His aunt had put fresh white oblong doilies on the dresser and table, a clean blue spread on the huge old mahogany bed, and crisp, filigreed curtains at the window. The throw-rug on the varnished floor, made by his grandmother from old stockings years ago, had been put through the washing machine. The two straw-bottomed chairs looked faded and forlorn, but he knew they also had been washed. He closed the expensive cowhide valise and locked it, put it on the floor, and sat on the bed beside his hat and topcoat.

The door opened and an elderly woman stuck her head inside. She wore a bandana that was wound about her head like a turban. "You 'bout ready?" she said. "Time aint long as it has been."

"Yes, I'm all set, Mrs. Henderson," he said.

Mrs. Henderson was housekeeper and practical nurse for his grandmother. Although old and toothless, she was still agile and strong, and the work was not difficult for her. She had only to make her ward as comfortable as was possible now, and keep the house tidy. Aunt Lou did the more thorough cleaning on the weekend.

"Mister Carl, let me tell you, you the spitting image of your Uncle Barnes," she said, closing her filmy eyes and smacking her lips. "Prettiest colored man I ever did see. You just like him, too."

He chuckled, unembarrassed. He knew he did not look like his uncle who, in any case, was not "pretty." His uncle had the light skin and the sharp, near-Nordic features of Carl's grandfather. Carl, on the other hand, had inherited his own father's bold features. And while he liked to think he was not unattractive, he knew very well that his face had the loose, slightly swollen and battered look of the prize-fighter. "She's buttering me up," he thought. And, to discourage her, he said nothing. He got out his cigarettes, put one between his lips and lit it.

"I hope you'll have just a minute to chat with me 'fore you go," she said more soberly, correctly interpreting his silence.

"Sure, Mrs. Henderson, I'll have time."

"Well, all right then, I'll leave you be." She withdrew her head and closed the door.

He let his eyes roam over the room again, wondering vaguely what Mrs. Henderson wanted to say to him. Then he forgot her, concentrating instead on the age-browned oval portrait of a young couple on the opposite wall. The man was stiffly handsome, his quadroon face chiseled. The woman was comely, dark and shy, and wore an improbably grotesque, high-crowned hat. It was a portrait of his grandparents taken after their wedding in the eighteen-eighties. "I never knew those people," he smiled wryly to himself.

Carl tried to remember how his grandparents had looked when his mother first brought him to live with them when he was five years old. He found that he remembered his grandmother with ease but that little else of that time was very clear in his mind. It had been a time of upheaval, confusion and sadness. He remembered his father's funeral only mistily, the gray casket in which he had lain so still, his black face ashened as though powdered, and the huge, box-like black hearse that took him away. His mother wept continuously, it had seemed, even when they moved out of the tall dark building where they had lived and took a train (it had been his first train ride), ending up in the unfamiliar place with the strange people who he learned where his grandparents.

He did remember vividly, however, his mother, still weeping, hurrying to the taxi waiting in front of the house, the driver carrying her bags and loading them on the back seat. She had squeezed and kissed him and told him to be good, and he understood she was going away without him. He became hysterical. His grandfather held him while he kicked and fought and screamed, until the car was out of sight and his mother was gone. In all the years afterwards he had not been fond of his grandfather, and now he wondered if that was perhaps the reason.

His image of his grandfather was of a wizened droopily mustached little man the color of sea-washed sand, with long, tangled gray-black hair that always need cutting. But that was how his grandfather had looked when he died thirteen years earlier, and he may not have looked that way thirteen years before that.

It was different with his grandmother. He would never forget anything about her. At the time of his first crisis, when he was uprooted and, he thought then, abandoned, she had been there to lessen his loneliness and desperation. She had replenished his plundered world with love. In those days she was a stately woman, sturdy and ample, with a round, sorghum-brown face. Her arms were large and strong and her bosom like a soft warm mountain. She was the most impressive person he had ever known, and there had been nothing in her rotund face and great bulk to link her with the svelte young woman in the photograph.

Time, inexorable and impersonal, had worked still another transformation, and the jolly woman of his childhood bore no resemblance to the gray, arthritic and age-wasted creature now lying asleep under the benevolence of drugs in the next room. The thought drew his face to the drab blue wall. He frowned unconsciously, expelling smoke from his lungs. In a little while he would hold her fleshless hand and speak with her (what could he say?) for the last time on this earth. He felt helpless and useless and, for the first time in his thirty-one years, knew the terrible simplicity of the inevitable.

Carl dislodged the somber reflection with a twist of his head. There would be plenty of time for philosophical musing on the plan. Now he felt he should be talking with Aunt Lou, deciding what was to be done. Surely, however delicate, such talk was appropriate. He got up, squashed the cigarette in the ashtray, and went out in the hallway. The floorboards grumbled under his weight. The corridor was narrow and dingy and smelled of closeness and the odor of freshly brewed coffee. "I guess Mrs. Henderson is having her umpteenth cup," he thought.

At the front of the house he peered into the living room, looking for Aunt Lou. She was not there. He lingered a moment in the doorway. This had once been his favorite of all rooms. He had no memory of the living room in his father's house, but he had many memories of this one. Had it changed much? The piano was still there, black and shiny, with the large tinted family portraits on top, though possibly not in the same place. Even then Aunt Lou was always changing the furniture around, lifting and shoving the divan and two armchairs while he rolled the carpet. Only the big upright Philco, with its stuck panel doors, had remained in the same spot because of all the wires behind it that ran through the window and down the side of the house. The Philco was gone now, and a television set and console record player were added, and probably the divan and chairs and the carpet were new. There was an artifical gas log fire installed in the fireplace where once real wood and coal had burned. He had sprawled in front of it evenings, listening to Little Orphan Annie and Dick Tracy on the radio or playing sultan to his grandmother's Scheherazade as she whisked him away to an exotic pastoral past where coiled rattlers lurked on the smokehouse floor and wily weasels terrorized the barnyard.

Smiling absently, he pushed open the screen door and walked onto the front porch. It was a sunny Georgia autumn afternoon, drowsily warm and crystal despite the gossamer shroud of dust over everything. The narrow, ell-shaped house across the unpaved street, originally white, was rouged with powdered earth. His grandmother's house, also white, was less stained as it stood yards from the street and was shielded from the pervading dust by the two giant oaks in the front lawn.

The dust never failed to depress him. An old bitterness revived and flowed through him everytime he turned off the main street of the town onto the street where his grandmother lived (He thought: "We have to spend so much of our energy in helpless anger.") For the first two blocks the street was wide and clean, lined with trees and big frame and brick houses. The pavement continued in the next block, but minus the cleanliness and order. The eroded sidewalks grew tangled weeds and bushes, and shabby shanties occupied by outcast whites sat back from the street, half-hidden behind wild chinaberry bushes and poplar trees. This was the buffer zone between the white people who mattered and the Blacks. Abruptly the pavement ended and the street was red clay, hard and dusty or soft and slushy, depending on the weather. The street improved slightly in his grandmother's block, where the handsomest homes of Blacks were located. Periodically, to pacify these taxpayers, the city spread over the street a layer of gravel. It promptly vanished in the mire when it rained. Only the next street was paved. It was the through-way to the all-white municipal golf course.

A blue sedan rolled slowly up the street and stopped in front of the house, dust billowing behind it. It was Aunt Lou's car. She climbed out and slammed the door and came toward him over the walkway from the cindered sidewalk. She was short and plump, as his grandmother had been at that age, with the same round face and skin the color of the browning leaves. "Hello," she greeted him in her low, tired voice. The voice now saddened him, for he recalled when it had been light and lilting. "Is Mama awake yet?" she asked, forcing a smile as tired and strained as her voice.

"No." He shook his head. He wished she would be gay. "Where'd you sneak off to?"

"To buy food. It's Saturday, you know." The words were a rebuff. "I was coming to ask you to bring the groceries in the house. It's not everyday there's a man around to do that. I might as well take advantage of it."

"Glad to oblige," he said.

He went out to the car and got the huge bags of groceries from the rear seat. When he came back up the walkway she had mounted the three steps to the terraced rock garden and was stooping over the oval-shaped fishpond, raking leaves to one corner with a stick. He put the groceries in one of the straw-bottomed rocking chairs on the porch and leaped over the cement balustrade and joined her in the garden. She twisted her thick neck to look up at him. "The water should be changed," she said, "but I'll wait until the leaves stop falling."

Carl watched her lifting the wet leaves from the pond with her pudgy fingers, her movements slow and awkward. His eyes strayed to her head. The thick hair was oiled and straightened, with feathers of gray in the black mass. He did not know what to say to her. Words had never flowed easily between them. Now, when it seemed really important, it was no easier than it had ever been. When he was a child she had been too busy to bother much with him. She was dedicated to her music, studying, planning and saving. One day she would throw up teaching school and sail to Italy to learn from the great vocal masters. She was too busy even for the men who had courted her--the young minister at the church, the male teachers at her school. When they came calling, she spent much of the time at the piano singing exuberantly, but more for her own pleasure than for theirs. They had not come to hear her sing.

Aunt Lou had once given him piano lessons. But she soon tired of it and sent him instead to another teacher in the next block. He had not liked the woman, and his musical education had ended quickly. He did not care. Music had seemed exciting only when he saw Aunt Lou at the piano, flashing her fingers over the keys and rousing the neighborhood with her arias.

Later, when he was again with his mother and his new

stepfather in Detroit, a recital was arranged for Aunt Lou at the Art Institute. She arrived in a plethora of excitement, and her radiance astonished him. She seemed for the first time to be beautiful. Her picture was in the papers and on posters announcing, "Louise Brady, lyric soprano." He was proud. His own Aunt Lou. But all went wrong. The audience was less than entranced and the critics in the newspapers were cruel. She had planned to stay in the city a week but instead went home the next day. And she never again appeared in a public recital.

He knew that disenchantment weighed heavy in her. Not merely because of the shadow now haunting her life. Death, the ultimate surrender, did not rank with the graver failures of spinsterhood and talent. It was rather that the intervals between great disillusions had been so rarely filled with joy. He wanted to say something cheerful. Or comforting, at least. But he could think of nothing that would not sound of pity. And pity would alarm and offend her, and the chasm between them would spread wider still.

"Do you remember how we used to empty the pond?" he asked.

She looked up at him again, cocking her head. "We? Who?"

"You and I."

She laughed softly, with surprise, not mirth, and dropped her head, shaking it. "No, I don't remember at all."

"Well, you showed me how," he said, kneeling beside her. "There was a piece of hose about six or seven feet long. I'd put one end in the bottom of the pond and suck through the other end. The water would start flowing up and out on the ground. I got a mouthful of dirty water every time."

She shook her head again. "No, I don't remember that.

It was awfully unsanitary. It might have made you sick."

"It takes more than a little dirty water to make little boys sick."

"I suppose so."

"I often think of some of the things I used to do back in those days. Things that would just about kill me now, I guess."

She stopped raking the leaves and stood up. She regarded him with an odd coldness, straightening the folds of her navy blue skirt. Despite her apparent lack of interest he went on talking, standing up beside her, looking down into her solemn face.

"I used to sneak off in the woods and go swimming with Sandy in the creek," he said. "You remember Sandy, my dog, I'm sure. Well, there were water moccasins around there, and minnows and tadpoles, the dog, and God alone knows what else. I guess I would swallow a gallon of that dirty water a day. The only bad after-effect, though, was the spanking I got when I got home. You probably don't remember. Mama could tell I'd been in the water. She always knew. I didn't understand until years later that she could tell because of the sand in my hair and the sandy ash on my face."

"Yes, it's easy to tell that way," she said and moved along the cobblestone path toward the house.

He remained still, watching her go, imagining her old and withered, a shawl about her shoulders, shambling among the jonquils and the dahlias and the tall sunflowers. He decided not to pursue her. Perhaps it was better to leave things as they were. She would make the necessary arrangements. Perhaps his efforts at intimacy only discomforted her.

Mrs. Henderson emerged onto the porch and crossed to the balustrade, motioning to him. "Is she awake?" he called out, a knot of anxiety leaping up in his throat.

"Naw, she still sleeping, Mister Carl," Mrs. Henderson said. "But I think you better come in her and have a bite to eat. You ought to have something in your stomach before you go away from here."

"I'm not hungry, Mrs. Henderson," he protested. "And I'll get a meal on the plane."

"Makes no difference," she persisted. "You come on in here and I'll make you some ham and eggs. You'll need it."

He knew it was useless to argue. She was determined to "chat" with him. At the steps to the porch he passed Aunt Lou and took the bag of groceries that Mrs. Henderson was trying to lift. "You're a little young for such a big load," he teased her. Mrs. Henderson held the door open. "I ain't young as I used to be, and that's for sure," she said. He entered the house behind Aunt Lou.

In the kitchen Carl sat at the table while Aunt Lou put the groceries away and Mrs. Henderson fussed at the gas range. "You feel like eating a mouthful, too?" she asked Aunt Lou. The offer was for the sake of courtesy.

"No, thank you," Aunt Lou replied remotely, moving ponderously about the room. When she had finished storing the groceries, she left without a word.

The kitchen was high-ceilinged, like the rest of the house, pine-paneled, and painted white. In recent years Aunt Lou had installed such modern conveniences as a deep freeze, walls of cabinets, and all manner of electrical mixers, squeezers and toasters. Mrs. Henderson did not know how to use many of the appliances and would not try to. "The old-fashioned way will do me till I die," she would say.

Now, frying the eggs, she repeated what she had already said to Carl at least a half dozen times in the past two days.

"Your grandma's so happy to see you, Mister Carl. It's done her old heart really good."

"Well, I'm glad," he said warily. He wished she wouldn't call him "mister," but she had ignored his suggestion that she call him Carl as she had always done. He supposed that she preferred to defer to his status as a "Northern professional man," which was her loose definition of his accountant job. "It's good to see her again too," he added.

"She always talks 'bout you," Mrs. Henderson declared. "A few weeks 'fore you come, she was telling me 'bout the time she made you go to the woods in the dark and bring that old dog back. Weak as she was, she bust out laughing. She said you was the scaredest little boy in Georgia that night. You remember that, Mister Carl?"

"Yes," he nodded, smiling. Yes, he remembered. It was one of his grandmother's favorite stories about him. It had been one of the few times she had severely punished him. He turned back through the clutter of his memory to that time. It stood out clearly among the years like a snapshot still black and white in an album of prints already faint and yellowed with age.

***

He had been seven or eight years old, for he could read the posted notices that all dogs not innoculated and tagged by a certain date would be taken by the dogcatcher. To punish him for some disobedience he could now no longer recall, his grandmother told him she would refuse to have Sandy innoculated, and none of his frantic entreaties could sway her. To his tearful vows to never disobey again, she remained obdurate. "You're not a good boy and you don't deserve a dog," was all she would say. On the eve of the deadline he conceived a desperate plan. In the woods where he and the dog went exploring was a tarpaper and pasteboard shack occupied by an eccentric but kindly man. The dog catcher would never go there. He took the big, cinnamon-colored German Shepherd to the shack and asked the old man if he could leave the dog there, promising to bring food everyday. The old man agreed. He tied the dog to a tree beside the shack and went home. His joy in saving the dog's life far outweighed his grief in having to leave him in so lonely a place.

After supper, when it was time to feed Sandy, Carl's grandmother became concerned at the animal's failure to appear. As dusk settled she went into the street, calling the dog's name. When he didn't come she decided he had been captured and prepared to go to the city pound to fetch him. At that point, with his conscience twisting him into an emotional rope, Carl confessed.

His grandmother was furious, more for being outwitted than anything else. After threatening to give him "the thrashing of your life," which is what he would have preferred, she hit upon a cleverer punishment. She sent him alone into the darknening woods to bring the dog home.

Carl started out bravely, for the walk to the edge of the woods held no terrors. But suddenly, confronted with the black and forbidding wall of trees and brush, his courage faltered. But he plunged in, futilely trying to shut out of his ears the eerie chirping of cicadas and crickets and the weird trumpeting of tree frogs. His ripe imagination littered the dark path with vicious, crawling reptiles and posted fierce, snarling leopards behind every bush. The woods that in the daytime beckoned with countless intriguing surprises now loomed and crackled like a leafy purgatory. He had not dreamed his grandmother capable of such cruelty.

The shack stretched an eternity away. When finally he approached it, he was running breathlessly along the path. He called out, tears burning his eyes, "Sandy, Sandy." The dog barked in the echoing night, straining at the rope. They collided with such force that he fell to the ground. The dog was all over him, crazy with eagerness. The paws scratched his arms; the hot tongue blinded him, lapping in his face. But he was far happier to see Sandy there in that forsaken place than the dog could possibly have been in seeing him.

***

"I guess that learned you all right," Mrs. Henderson said, grinning, nodding her bandanaed head. "I guess you behaved yourself after that."

His reminiscent smile widened. "That was the only time in my life I ever hated her," he said. "Especially when I found out she had already had the dog innoculated. I really hated her. If I hadn't just had a terrible time in the woods, I think I would've run away."

Mrs. Henderson cackled. "No, I dare say you never could hate your grandma, Mister Carl. Not you. Not for nothing. She always pinned her hopes on you. After Mister Wesley died, and there was no man around this house, she used to say you was coming back here when you finished your education. 'Carl will come and look after his old grandma's place,' she used to say. 'My little Carl is coming back.' That's what she used to say all the time."

He stared at the old woman with something close to revulsion, as though really seeing for the first time how unlovely she was. She was ochre-colored, with the sharp features and long face of her Anglo-Saxon forebears, and her skin was ash-dry and withered. She was tall, thin, and bent, and her long blue frock touched the tips of her shoes. She wore a faded oxford-gray sweater and a clean white apron that looped over her neck and waist. "She's like some old voodoo witch," Carl thought.

She brought a plate of fried ham and eggs and put it in front of him. Then, moving about with unexpected sprightliness, she provided him with silverware and two slices of toast. "Go ahead and eat," she commanded. "The coffee'll be ready in a minute."

He hadn't told her he wanted coffee, and would've preferred milk, but he said nothing. When she placed a cup and saucer beside his place and put another cup and saucer opposite him, he understood why he was going to have coffee. "This looks good," he said appreciatively, and started to eat.

When the coffee was ready. Mrs. Henderson filled the two cups and sat across from him. She put three heaping teaspoons of sugar in her cup and stirred it slowly. "A big, strapping, fine-looking man like you ought to eat," she said. "You can't depend on that little sandwich they give you in the airplane."

"They don't give you a sandwich," he said. "You get a complete meal." Well, I don't see how they can give nobody no food in that little old airplane up in the air." She raised a bony hand in a nebulous gesture, dismissing the subject. She shifted her body in the chair and sipped the coffee, pursing her loose thin lips into a funnel like the tip of an elephant's trunk. She swallowed the coffee, wiped her mouth with the back of her hand and pointed herself at him. "Mister Carl, maybe I oughtn't talk so much,' cause it ain't none of my business. But I been knowing all your family since Heav'n knows when, and I'm just going to speak my mind.

"That poor old soul laying in yonder, she don't like having to go on to her reward and leaving this house and her land here with no man to look after it. That's what's worrying her weary old mind more'n anything. Other'n that, she could just go in peace with nary a sorrow. She's lived a good life, Josie Brady has. A good life. Never harmed a soul. Why, I recollects way back 'fore your own Ma come into the world, long 'fore Miss Louise was thought of, Miss Josie worked all day in the white folks' house, cleaning and scrubbing, and all through the night, sometimes till daybreak the next day, working by lamplight, she was washing and i'ning clothes for the white folks. That's the way she got the money to send your Ma and Miss Louise and your two uncles to school. Mister Wesley, he worked true, and he worked hard at the terra cotta factory till he was too old for that sort of work. But it was that poor old soul who was at it night and day, cooking and cleaning and washing and i'ning till her back was fit to break. And all the young'uns 'cept Miss Louise, they all went on up North after she done worked and slaved to give 'em a education. That's what they did. All 'cept Miss Louise, and she stayed."

Mrs. Henderson paused long enough to refuel her lungs then went on. "But now, I might as well just say it, Mister Carl. I might as well speak my mind now 'cause it'll be too late after you gone. Miss Louise stayed on good and loyal to mind her Ma, but she ain't got no man, and she aint no man herself, and so that don't help the matter none at all. That don't put that old soul's mind not a bit more at ease. It hurt her so to think this house and this land is gong to be sold or somebody she don't know nothing 'bout will have it after she gone. It hurt her to her soul. And it just don't seem right she got to go away from here with no satisfaction in her mind."

The food stuck in his throat. He washed it down with the strong, hot, bitter coffee. He stared hard at the old woman unsubtly accusing him of betrayal. But, realizing that his irritation showed in his face, he glanced away from her toward the window. The pecan, wild cherry and peach trees were in rows on the lots behind the house. Weeds grew rampant on the uncultivated ground that had always been planted with vegetables when his grandfather lived. He turned back to his plate, but the sight of the food repelled him. He wouldn't be able to eat it now. He was irritated with himself for allowing the busybody crone to scuttle his equanimity.

Carl drank the coffee and excused himself over Mrs. Henderson's objections. He left the kitchen by the rear door and went down the steps into the back yard. Crab grass and weeds grew everywhere, around the garage, between the rocks of the paths leading to the wire-enclosed chicken yard and to the peach orchard. He noticed several fat, listless hens waddling behind the wire. He recalled with a pang the flocks of white leghorns and Rhode Island Reds his grandfather had kept. He turned from that side of the house, as if fleeing the memory, and walked back in front of the garage toward the street.

At the edge of the driveway he stopped and faced the house. It was wide and flat, with a red roof that slanted at a low angle. A basement had been dug long after the house was built and the brick wall at the base was newer than the pillars. The hedges that hemmed the property were high and in need of trimming, as were the oak trees and the conglomeration of cedars and shrubs that obscured the porch. He recalled Aunt Lou, in a long ago fervor of landscaping, planting the cedars and later hanging them with lights at Christmas. The fenced-in vacant lots on both sides of the house and the rock garden, now clay-sterile and ragged with weeds and tough grass, belonged to his grandmother too. She had had the strength to gain it. Did her progeny have the strength to keep it?

Carl experienced a spasm of regret. He dug his hands in his pockets and gazed at the ground. In the distance children laughed, their voices mingling with the cackling of hens and the roar of motors on the busy street a block away. All the sounds seemed to converge and riot in him, catalyzing his private turmoil. Regret, kindled by a haunting, inadmissable guilt, burned into shackled rage.

He raised his face from the ground and swore, "Dammit, dammit!" and hustled up the sidewalk, angling in the walkway to the front steps. He sat on the concrete balustrade and nursed his simmering frustration. He could never live here. His grandmother knew he could never live here now. It had been different as a child. But even at ten, his mother had decided it was time for him to leave ("Why, the child can't even use the public library," she explained to his grandmother). He had promised he would be back, but he did not know what a difference time would make. How could he have known? None who had left could return. Didn't she know that? Did she think his mother and his uncles merely callous and contrary? Didn't she know they had made a step forward, a step nearer the goal she had herself set for them? Wouldn't it be betraying her not to seek a fuller freedom? (No, they were not free! Not truly free! But they were freer than they could be here.) And, after all, what could he do in that sullen, cheerless place choked by disdain and red dust? Nothing had changed. He still couldn't use the public library.

The screen door opened and Aunt Lou stepped onto the porch behind him. He turned, greeting her appearance with anxious relief. He saw that her eyes were red as if from weeping and that a tight line angled down from the corners of her mouth.

"She's awake now," she said, averting her eyes. "She's still under the drugs but Mrs. Henderson will keep her from falling asleep for a few minutes. You'd better go now. I'll wait in the car to drive you to the airport. You can bring your suitcase out when you're ready."

Her voice seemed soft, tender, and he thought: "She's talking to me as though I am a child."

He stood up and went toward her, looking squarely into her face, searching it for a sign. For a moment their eyes met, and in that moment he raised his arms to grasp her shoulders and to pull her to him. But she moved quickly, clumsily, beyond his reach. He remained frozen in the half-completed gesture, looking foolish, and feeling it. After a moment he dropped his arms and shrugged in defeat. Then he opened the screen door.

"There's just this one thing!" she said suddenly, her voice strangled with emotion. Her eyes were riveted on the balustrade, her fists were clenched. "You can't love her into Heaven now. You weren't here when she needed you. There was no man here. It's too late to love her now, it's too late."

She raised her face to confront him then, fury flaming in her watering eyes. But it was an impersonal fury, or an all-encompassing fury, flaring through him at some greater target. "Mama's going to die. Do you understand what that means? Nothing can keep her from dying, and you can't get any last minute stars in your crown by making her think you love her so much. You come here now, with her on her deathbed, and you think you're going to get automatic redemption for all the years you didn't even come here to see her. I heard Mrs. Henderson. Yes, I heard her. But let me tell you. And you can tell your mother and all the others. You can tell them. I wasted my life here. While they were out in the world doing what they wanted to do, I was here. I gave up everything to stay here. I could have gone away too. I could have been a great singer. I could have married. Yes, I could have married many times. But I stayed here. I was here when Papa died, and I'll be here when Mama dies. None of the others will. You won't. You'll all come running back to the funeral, mourning and crying and pretending you cared so much. Well, it's no good. It won't make any difference. It's all over now."

Carl stared at her, appalled. He would not have been more shocked had she suddenly stripped naked before him. At first he did not comprehend. He could not believe. But then, watching as she fumbled in her jacket pocket for her handkerchief and stumbled toward the stairs in movements redolent of a weariness complete and profound, he understood at last the abyss between them. He knew now how her emptiness had been filled. She hurried down the stairs and out to the street, climbing in the car and slamming the door. She collapsed over the steering wheel, her body shaking as she wept.

Carl went inside the house and walked down the dim, musky hallway to his grandmother's room. He paused a moment with his hand on the doorknob. This was the moment he had dreaded. But now, somehow, inexplicably, it would be less difficult to face.

Dusk

Brian Ray

The sun was casting long shadows across the sidewalks and alleys. It hung slightly above the hazy horizon, lingering like the last few licks on a lollipop. Chicago was not living up to its nickname of the Windy City today, not even a trace of a breeze was in was in the air. The day had settled, bloomed and was beginning to fold.

Grasshoppers were out and Isaac wanted to catch one. He wanted to hunt them down in the prairie reclaimed vacant lot two blocks over. A few years ago an apartment building burned down there, leaving its shell. The walls remained for a short while before they fell down too. By the next summer, weeds, grass, and grasshoppers were plentiful in the space.

From his bedroom window Isaac could not see the lot. He could see the alley, garages and garbage cans, and an occasional car. He could see the back porches of other apartment buildings just like his. Without wanting to, he could see the people in these places.

Isaac watched as a tall thin man and a shorter thin woman walked through the back gate and up the walk. He could barely hear them plod up the back steps. Within less than two minutes, they were on their way out of the yard, more links in the unending chain of pipeheads that came through once or twice a day. Scandalous, the dealer on the first floor, had been selling rock bags all summer. Isaac figured Scandalous had made enough money today to probably pay rent for the whole building.

A basketball began its rhythmic striking on the alley

pavement. It was followed by the voices of three or four boys. No one Isaac knew, but then there were always people around here he didn't know. They must have been from the block across the alley. For a moment he thought one of them might be Dinky, but it wasn't. Dinky was over at his cousin's house on the West Side, but then again he should be home by now, school was starting in two weeks.

His mother was in the next room singing along to some song that was playing on the radio. She was probably cleaning up, the only thing she really liked to do. Isaac returned to looking out of the window, his face long in the edges of sunlight.

He heard the front door open and a man's voice. It was a voice he was not familiar with. Then his mother laughed. The laughter brought a smile to his face, then he heard it again, then the man's voice. Isaac got off the bed and walked to the door, carefully stepping over the toys that were on his bedroom floor. He stopped for a moment at the door, listening for the voice again. Instead he heard his mother call him.

Isaac slowly stepped into the living room, his head down. This time the voice seemed to boom, "Looks like he's gonna be a ball player."

Isaac looked up, way up, the man must have been well over six feet. Isaac was not yet five feet high. His mother was still smiling, not the smile Isaac was used to. Not the smile of a good grade, or a paper heart, a totally different smile.

"Bobby, this is my son Isaac. Isaac, this is my friend Bobby."

Isaac looked at the giant of a man. His chest was broad, wide shoulders, he had honey colored skin, and very white teeth. The man had on a pair of jeans and a tee shirt. Isaac said a low, "Hello."

"Aw, it ain't got to be like that."

Isaac regarded the man again. It was not that the man was menacing; even though he was towering over him Isaac just didn't know him or what to make of him. The man spoke again. "You ever been to a baseball game?"

Isaac looked up to his smiling face once again. "No."

"Well, I'll tell you what, I know you'll be starting school in a couple of weeks, and the White Sox are gonna be in the playoffs this year, so if you bring home one 'A' paper then I'll take you to a playoff game."

Isaac thought about this deal for a moment. "What if I get a 'B'?"

"Then I'll take you, but I won't bring you back."

The man smiled, then Isaac smiled. The man stuck his hand out. "Is it a deal?"

"All I got to get is one 'A' paper, right?"

"Before the Sox win the World Series this year."

Isaac shook Bobby's extended hand and smiled. "I can do that. Can't I mama?"

His mother smiled. "Yes I know you can, as a matter of fact he'll probably have to take you to a couple of games."

Bobby looked at Isaac and winked, "That's all right, I got season tickets."

Isaac watched his mother standing closer to Bobby than she was to him. He watched as her eyes twinkled while she smiled, the same smile since Bobby had come in. Bobby reached in his pocket and pulled out his wallet. He looked through the wallet and pulled out some money. He rolled off three dollars and handed them to Isaac. "Here, go get yourself some comic books or something."

Isaac's mother started to intercept the money, when

Bobby held the money closer to Isaac, but he spoke to Isaac's mother, "I ain't giving this to you, I'm giving it to him."

"It's not the money, I mean I don't mind him having money. I don't know. It's just that I don't want him out there running the streets or nothing like that."

Bobby, still smiling his smile said, "He can take care of himself, he'll be fine."

Isaac's mother slowly withdrew her hand, letting it fall to her side. Isaac reached up and took the three dollars. He smiled at Bobby, the big giant of a man. Bobby returned the smile, and Isaac's mother was silent.

"Make sure you have your key."

The screen door slammed shut, and Isaac was running down the back stairs. He slowed down as he ran past Mrs. Handley's porch, stopping to listen to see if there was anyone below him; and on Scandalous' porch he hesitated again.

He cautiously walked through the yard of brown grass and dirt until he got to the back gate. At the back gate he stopped and listened; hearing nothing, he ran down the alley.

He came out of the alley at 47th street, turning right at the corner. Forty-seventh street always seemed to call for an extreme amount of caution on his behalf. He wound his way through shoppers, old drunk men, and teenagers.

The teenagers scared him the most. They were menacing, standing around with their hats cocked to the side. They always stood in groups of two or three. As often as he had been down 47th Street, none of them had really ever seemed to notice him. Still he felt unable to take a chance on them.

There were two blocks between him and the candy store. He slowed down as he reached the corner with the vacant lot. There were all sorts of men in that lot, sitting around, never seeming to do anything in particular. Some of them had even brought chairs to sit on. He thought about stopping to look for grasshoppers, but the men seemed to have staked their claim on the lot.

Once while walking by them one of them asked him to go to the store across the street to get cigarettes for him. Isaac almost froze not knowing what to do. "I ain't getting you nothing," Isaac had said before running off.

Isaac looked into the vacant lot, seeing the men there he slowed down even more. He tried to appear nonchalant as he walked by. His heart was beating fast and hard, and he was sure someone would see it through his shirt.

Once at the corner he looked both ways. Not seeing any cars coming, he ran across the street.

Isaac looked into the tall store windows as he passed them, stopping once to look at a radio controlled car in the window of the beauty supply store. Isaac's fingers hesitated on the window above the car. He tapped it twice and ran his fingers over the length of the window as he walked off.

On the corner two old ladies stood waiting for a bus. They were huddled in fear, hoping that they could go unnoticed by everyone else on the street. A bus heaved its way down the street in the opposite direction. Music came blaring out of the speaker over the record store. The barbecue shack poured smoke out over the street.

Across the street in front of the liquor store some men stood around, idly walking circles in front of the door. One would sit on the garbage can, talking to and occasionally pointing at the others.

Women walked up and down the street; small children all around them, arms outstretched begging to be picked up. The children's faces were an unequal mixture of dirt, syrup from candy and IceCees, sweat and tear stains. The same things in different proportions could be found on their shirts and hands. The mother, usually with one child already riding her hip, paid no attention to the pleas, and they urged the children to keep up the pace and stay together.

Isaac walked slowly into the candy store. There were a couple of older boys that he didn't know in the doorway. He wished they weren't there and that he didn't have to see them. The boys looked at him and let him pass.

He ran to the counter since there was no one there in line. "Can I have some uh, some uh..."

He looked into the taped glass counter for something that he wanted. ".....Now & Laters."

The old lady never looked away from the small black and white television at the end of the counter. "What kind you want, baby?"

She adjusted the twisted coat hanger to stop the picture from fuzzing up. "What kind you got?" Isaac asked now looking at bubble gum.

"Oh, we got all of 'em, we got the banana-strawberry, we got all of 'em." She turned and looked at Isaac through the bulletproof glass.

"Well, let me have some Hot Cheezlets and some Salt and Sour, and five wine candies, five mint juleps, and a pack of chocolate Now and Laters."

The old lady gathered the candy together and punched a cash register. "That will be eighty-one cents."

"I thought they was a quarter a piece."

"They are but you got to add tax, so then its eighty-one cents."

Isaac passed a crumpled dollar through the slot in the window. The lady took the money from him. "I'ma put the change in the bag, okay?"

Isaac passed the other dollar through the slot. "Can I have four quarters for a dollar, please?"

"Okay, baby."

She pulled the dollar through the slot, then put four more quarters in the bag. She placed the bag on the bulletproof glass-enclosed lazy susan. Isaac reached up and pulled the bag out, peered into it and picked out all the candy, stuffing it into his pockets. With his goodies properly divided and stashed, he approached the row of video games on the other side of the store.

He dropped a quarter into a slot, intending to play all four games. For the next fifteen minutes he beat up, shot and exterminated all kinds of villains. When his quarters were exhausted he left the store.

Isaac began the trip home, back down the street and up the alley. He stopped and listened at the gate. When he was sure he had heard nothing he walked toward the back porch. As he approached the bottom steps, he heard someone on the porch. From the first step he looked toward the drug dealer's apartment. There were three men on the porch.

Isaac took a silent step backward. At first he wanted to run back toward the alley, but then they might see him. He decided to go down to the basement door. He knew he would be directly under them, but they wouldn't be there long.

Gingerly holding the bag with just his forefinger and thumb, he crept down the steps to the basement doorway. He hesitated momentarily giving thought to the chance that a rat or two might already be down there. After briefly weighing the alternative he went ahead down the concrete steps, into the cool dark doorway.

Isaac was taking slow breaths, as he listened to the men

talking to each other. They were directly over him. He could hear them talking, but could not understand what they were saying.

From inside the apartment the door opened, some words were passed. Isaac tried not to pay attention to what they were saying, but he could hear them speaking in muffled tones, sort of like a television in the next room.

He sat wishing he could get into his potato chips. He figured since he wasn't doing anything else, he could go on and eat his chips. Because he didn't want the men over him to hear him, he tried not to make any noise.

He had lots of practice for this feat, eating chips and candy in school. First he had to get the bag open, being careful not make any noise. He pulled the bag apart, starting in the middle, real slow. His mouth was starting to water in anticipation of the potato chips. This made them even better, that he had to go through all this to eat them. So, consumed in the opening of the bag, he temporarily forgot about the men standing over him.

Flash boom, flash boom, flash boom. He saw the first flash out of the corner of his eye. He jumped, spilling the potato chips. He looked directly up seeing the second and third shot. Watching, in what seemed like slow motion, as one of the men on the porch fired the shots. Even with his ears ringing, he heard the thud on the floor inside the apartment.

He could hear some running from inside the apartment. Another shot from inside the apartment, some more running, then another shot. Then there was a thud on the porch; then someone ran down the steps, closely followed by someone else.

Whatever fell on the porch was blocking the light. For a long moment there was silence. The ringing was fading in his ear. Isaac heard drops hit the concrete around his feet.

He looked down expecting to see the blood gathered in a pool around his feet, but he could see nothing in the darkness. He was frozen in the corner, wanting desperately to run. Above him he heard Hrs. Handley scream.

The police would be there in a while. He had to get out before the police got there, they might want him to be a witness and testify, or something like that.

He could ear his own heartbeat echoing in his head. He tiptoed two steps forward. When he heard nothing, he continued. Finally he was out from under the porch. He started to go up the steps, but stopped when saw the dead man on the first floor.

The man faced Isaac--at least what was left of his face.

Half of his head was missing, parts of the eye still were visible. His brain and shards of his skull and facial muscles were well behind him on the wall and the steps going up. A deep chill ran up Isaac's spine, he felt himself starting to gag, and pulled his eyes away from the image.

Isaac looked into the apartment. There was Scandalous laying in the doorway. Isaac looked at the three holes in his back. They looked like little red explosions. Once again the chill came, but he didn't gag. The idea that he would never forget this scene flashed in his mind.

Isaac came down the steps and went into the front. He thought about how his mother would get mad at him when he rang the doorbell, but there was no way he could go up the back porch. He fingered the key in his pocket.

Dinky was across the street on the curb so Isaac went over there. As soon as he had shaken Dinky's hand, they both heard the sirens in the distance. The flashing lights from the police car jumped onto the street. The car sped around the corner almost hitting Mr. Simmons' old pickup truck. It was quickly followed by another, then two more. An ambulance screamed onto the street.

A crowd gathered, people wondering what happened. Isaac's mother and Bobby came out. His mother looked at Isaac, it was the look that always preceded her calling him. She took the customary breath and Isaac's name came out of her mouth. She rolled her eyes on to someone standing nearer to her.

Isaac felt a tinge of superiority as the stretchers were being carried out with the body bags on them. He had seen them before the police did, before anyone did. Anyone except the people that did the shooting. A chill ran down his spine as he remembered that someone did this, it was not a monster, but someone. To Isaac it was like being in a movie.

Isaac watched the stretchers being put into the ambulance; as it shrieked and wailed away, he put his hands into his pockets. Just as his fingertips touched the cellophane wrappings, he remembered the candy. He freed one from his pocket, unwrapped it and popped it into his mouth.

He rolled the piece of hard candy around in his mouth, before stuffing it into his cheek. "I saw both of them. Scandalous got shot three times in the back; the other one got his face, his whole head blown off," he said to Dinky.

Dinky didn't believe him, but just the same he would back him up to everybody at school.

Isaac's mother shot a glance from across the street that told him it was time to come home. Isaac stepped off the curb; he looked down at the ground to make sure he wasn't stepping into something.

There on his white gym shoe were three drops of blood, one big one and two smaller ones. Isaac stopped almost halfway between the curb and the street. He started shoving Dinky to get his attention. "L-l-look Dinky, it's his blood o-on my shoe!" Dinky's mouth dropped.

Even with the sun almost down, already behind all the buildings across the street, Dinky could see the blood on Isaac's shoe. The street lights started blinking on, one by one, the blood blinked back on the shoe. Dinky turned and ran into his building.

"Isaac, come on now, time to go in," his mother shouted from across the street.

Isaac looked at his shoe once more; this time there was no chill. He ran across the street to his mother's side, the syrup from the penny candy filling his cheek.

Divine Days: Galloway Wheeler

Leon Forrest

The story was this: Once upon a time Galloway Wheeler was an assistant professor at main-line Negro college, in the English Department, where he taught Shakespeare. He had received the benefit of appointment and anointment by the direct hand of that prestigious educator, President Broadus Bluestone Bynum. Old B.B.B. was an old friend and rumored lover of Galloway's grand-aunt, who hailed from Virginia Negro aristocracy of 'black blue-bloods,' as the Shakespearean scholar dubbed them.

Notorious for the pauper's attire he wore to class, Wheeler turned out to be an excellent teacher, and not surprisingly, a very thorough and demanding instructor. It was said by many students that he actually breathed new life into the Bard's works, because of the intelligence and animated spirit he brought to his daily lectures and discussions.

However, being a bachelor at the time, Galloway Wheeler was also engaged in an attempt to live the full life of a single man, as much as his tiny salary at this Negro college would allow. In fact, he had come up with a most unique way of trying to supplement his monthly stipend from the school.

When Galloway ran up a flock of bills in town to the "embarrassment of the school," the President ordered Wheeler to report to his office at high noon, with his monthly budget in hand, itemizing "the nuts and bolts, the dollars and cents of every expenditure, so that I can set up an allowance schedule for you that you can live by, and one that shall not, and will not embarrass the credit arrangements that this temple of matriculation has set-up with the established enterprises in town." Wheeler was to "breathe not a word," about the Presidential summons to any living person, "so help you God."

President Bynum (who was proclaimed by certain students as Broad Bad Butt, kick-ass no chaser, or simply Buster Bull Balls) had Galloway kneeling on the luxurious Egyptian carpet in his offices, pleading for deliverance, after a time.. B.B.B. had one of those twelve column accounting statement forms out plotting how Wheeler might move from galloping deficit to solvent living. The miracle is of course that B.B.B. really liked Wheeler (and was still smittened by Wheeler's great-aunt, Doycelene). Of course old B.B.B. was known for his grandiloquent oratory; and his fondness for quoting from Shakespeare during his addresses and public pronouncements. So, there stood Wheeler, all six-feet of him, weighing about 139 pounds, soaking wet.

President Broadus Bluestone Bynum began calmly enough: "First off Wheeler, as a very junior professor, you must learn to avoid ostentatious living, at all costs. Your heritage is one resplendent with dignity. And as a consequence, you must learn to curb you appetites, lest you continue to bring shame upon this revered shrine of matriculation. Wheeler? Look to Falstaff. Never forget the Shakespearean warning to us all through the comportment and corpulence of Falstaff. Never forget Falstaf Ps gluttony. G for gluttony. Write that down, in your notebook, young, extremely junior professor Wheeler. Not G for Good. Always connect up G for Gluttony. Not G for Galloway."

"Yes, Sir," Wheeler said, as if he were reciting Nevermore, as he put pen to paper.

"Next, how do you spend out your monthly salary of

$199.99. A handsome stipend, I might add. Let me see your budget. What's this? $75.00 for spirits. $75.00 for foodstuffs? $4.00 clothing allowance. $20.00 for cleaning. $21.00 for books. $4.00 for carefree pleasures of the heart. No wonder your attire is renowned for its bohemian baggey buttness. I see before my eyes 'carefree pleasures of the heart.' My God Wheeler your stipend is not based upon your reckless spending. You'll be in an early grave brought on through the vicissitudes of high living. And oh my dear, I observe a flagrant but ample absence of any plan for Savings. That most cherished of all American institutional practices. Savings, man! God Galloway you need a wife to wheel your bold butt in. To stream-line your beefy living upon a rack of refining discipline.(Ah I like that phrase, too.) Have you no rectitude? No shame?

"Wheeler, you embarrass my faith in your sagacity. Priorities Wheeler. You've allowed riotous budgeting to turn your breeding into the mind-set of a vagabond, a drifter. And after I had told your dearly beloved Aunt that I would look out after you. Wheeler, priorities are pivotal to the fall or rise of any man's personal economy. To say nothing of that of a nation's decline, or the rise of an institution of higher learning. But must I lecture on this imperial theme to a would-be-scholar of Shakespeare? Your priorities are in reverse order. You've thrown the stick-shift of your automotive enterprise into reverse, even as you think you are going full speed ahead. Wheeler, you make your bed and you snore in it, remember that. And I could let it go at that, but there is this deeply implanted soul of integrity in me that demands I save you from yourself. Have you not considered Polonius here and his advice to Hamlet...And don't forget those immortal words of the Bard, 'put money in thy purse,' too."

This was the exact moment when Wheeler fell to the floor, upon his knees. Bynum no doubt thought it was out of humility, before the authority of Presidential truth and seal. The President said nothing, for this fall was fitting, especially for one who has fallen from grace. Wheeler started to say something about the President's references, (but said nothing, even though he was fairly floored by the Presidential abuses of the Bard's words) especially when he reconsidered the actual dust in his own pocket.

"A free-wheeler of here and there and every...Wait a moment, my God Galloway what in the hell do you do for shelter? Man, my God. You do need a wife. Where do you live? In the park? Are you a gate-keeper at the zoo? Or, are you shacking up with some wench colored-ill, by the cloak of night, under the stained sheets of immorality? How do you live in a shelter where there is no rent to be paid? Are you a professor without lodgings? Have you been sleeping after-hours in your classroom, for extra-credit, shall we say? Are we to refer to you as Professor Hapless, as well, as Professor Hopeless? Tenured in some temple of sin? Speak the speech man, trippingly, before the tides of my wrath...leap from my silver-tongue. Fool, where do you lay your burden down at night? In a distillery?"

Wheeler spoke barely above a whisper, meekly and humbly:

"In a coffin, Sir."

"WHAT?"

"...Well, Sir, you see.

"A Professor of mine in a coffin! Before his time. Arise up off your knees. Are you practicing for the gravedigger's role in Hamlet, after you're fired from this citadel of learning?"

"Wheeler, don't play with me, for if I do look like Othello

to you, you surely are no Iago in my imaginative reality."

"You see, Sir, on my sal, or stipend, President Bynum, Sir. Why I can't afford an insurance policy, nor an extra can of sardines."

"What about sen-sen for your bad breath?"

"I work for Lamb and Blake Mortuary. I mean I keep an eye on their funeral home by night, so nobody can steal bodies. And as you know, body snatchers abound. My pay--or I should say my keep is a free cushiony bed. I mean the narrows of a coffin are as comfortable as a bed of roses...Is always there because there always is a free coffin to go around. I keep the candles lit by the coffin at night so as I can bone-up on my Shakespeare, even as I am doing my chore as night-watchman at the funeral home."

Looking aghast as a shell-shocked ghost hit by an electrical bolt of lightning, President Bynum ran Wheeler not only out of his office, and off the campus, but chased the junior professor down the pebble-strewn paths, out on the road; the very tails of his blue-black Presidential morning coat flying in the wind. Meantime the school securitiy guards gave chase to them both fearing a Presidential heart-attack would occur, on their watch, as the President chased a professor. Then too, Bynum was in his late-sixties, and so the security guards were heard howling: "We'll catch him, Sir, just let us do the job, Mr. President."

By now classes were exiting. Students were gathering. One student was heard to exclaim: "Galloway's actually outrunning God, himself." Soon the students were giving chase, which made it appear as if the students were chasing the security police, who were chasing the President chase down a professor.

Broadus Bluestone Bynum remained oblivious to his

pursuers, screaming over and over again, after the assailant of propriety: "Out out damned spot. You are an idiot signifying nothing."

As it turned out old B.B.B. was chasing Wheeler down to the graveyard; but he didn't know this because actually Wheeler had nimbly come up with a cunning ruse. When he discovered where they were headed (not the railroad station) B.B.B. screamed: "Any spook this crazy has got to return to the graveyard and haunt his birth place. You galloping haint. Go haunt the graveyard. Damn if you'll haunt my campus."

Because you see Wheeler was never seen again on campus, not actually. The myth among the students was this: anybody who acted out, and got into trouble, but then was able to slip out of the straps of danger, by some clever ruse, or bold stratagem, was said to have been aided by "the galloping ghost of Galloway."

Or, if you were pledging a fraternity--on the other hand--and you screwed up, you were placed in a coffin, as one who is placed in a penalty box, during a game of hockey, for infraction of the rules. You had to stay there for twenty-four hours. In this way Wheeler's presence still haunts Bynum's college, even though professor Wheeler never received tenure. His tale has become a bedtime story all over the campus, in one manifestation, or another. During the early days of the Movement, it was rumored that one of the student demands might be that the administration accord an honorary degree to Wheeler, as Doctor of Divinity, with the inscription: "To the Man Who Out Ran God, once upon a time..."

And the branches of the Wheeler legend were everywhere. If you were trying to make it with a co-ed, but you didn't have money to take her out, she'd say well, if you really loved me, you'd take a job sleeping in a coffin at Lamb and Blake's, in order to save up for a date. Or, if a co-ed went out on a date with a guy, and it turned out to be really "dead" the young lady would say of her date that he was a "coffin stiff", or a "coffin corpse."

Popular professors who were up for tenure--but were involved in what appeared to be a losing battle were often referred to as not being in limbo, but rather that their petition was in "coffin's corner."

Gamey, if vulgar fraternity guys, often proclaimed their successful sexual escapades, in the following language: "I cut her in a coffin." And if the action was really fierce, a guy might declare: "I cut her on the killing ground; coffin, trimmings, and all."

Now you may well ask how the students found out the particulars of what went down in President Bynum's office? Well, according to Galloway Wheeler he typed up the whole story (apparently) duplicated about fifty copies, and placed them under the doors of dorms, late at midnight, seven days after this confrontation between President and Professor occurred. How did he get back on campus? This Wheeler never revealed.

Aunt Eloise said it was believed that the ghost of Galloway Wheeler had galloped back on campus after midnight, because a riderless horse was spotted by a co-ed, as she returned from a rendezvous, about 1:30. Since the co-ed was breaking curfew, and had to slip into the dorm through a secret passageway, she had to keep this aspect of the Galloway Wheeler saga secret and hidden, and only whispered to a few friends, and newspaper people, in cities, where alums of the school, like Aunt Eloise resided, but she didn't make her calls until after she had graduated.

The segment of 'the true story' that Wheeler wanted recited went this way: he had ducked President Bynum by hiding behind a large gravestone, in the white section of the cemetery. Afraid that he might be arrested for entering the white section of the bone-yard, the President of the Negro College, stopped at the separating line. But Wheeler reported how Bynum screamed out: "I knew this nigger was crazy. He's allow that Shakespeare to go to his head...Then I found out he was a spook, for real. Now I find out that Wheeler truly believes he's a white spook. I'm going home and get down on both of my knees and pray for the sanity of the race...pray to the Holy Ghost for deliverance."

Then at midnight Wheeler hid himself in a deep underground enclave, used as a station on the Underground Railroad, by escaping slaves. After the Civil War, this area of chosen earth was set aside and cordoned off as the cemetery of the colored populace. Wheeler hid himself there for a time, coming out only when he typed up the report of his interview with the President, and spreading the message beneath the doors of fifty of his favorite students.

Sweet Jesus Club

Sandra Jackson-Opoku

I'm writing all this stuff down. Every bit of it.

You ever write things down? I do it all the time when things get heavy on my mind. Not write them *up*, like you do with homework and stuff. I write them down so I can get it off my mind and on the paper where I can take a good look at them.

Like, for instance last Sunday, when Reverend Wesley said we must always count our blessings. Well, I don't have that many of them to count. So I've been counting my curses, too. Been making two lists. First one, all the things that are right with my life; a pretty short list. Second one, all the things wrong with it. I filled up both sides of a sheet of notebook paper and still ain't finished. Only reason I stopped is because it's time for me to get up and fix dinner for Mama and Benny.

Benny, my big brother, he's retarded. He don't talk much. He's been standing in front of the refrigerator for about five minutes now, just bouncing like he's got to go to the bathroom. The deeper his knee bends, the hungrier he's getting. Benny always be hungry. I wonder if they even feed him at that special education school he goes to. When the bus drops him off here at four, first thing he does is run in here looking for something to cram in his mouth. That boy is always eating.

But don't get me wrong. I'm crazy about Benny. He's more like a little brother than a big one, what with him being retarded and all. I'll take up for him in a minute. Nobody better not be trying to mess with my brother or they ass is grass.

It's just that I don't see why Mama's always got to have him hanging around my neck. I ain't but twelve and a half, and these are the best years of my life. All right, so Mama works two and three jobs and there ain't nobody else here to mind him. All that work, she still don't never have no money. So I don't see what the deal is. Anyway, that's why Benny winds up on both my lists. He's a blessing and a curse. Right now Mama's only on one of them. The long one.

"Pancakes." Benny squeezes up under my arm, peeping up in the refrigerator. "Eggs."

"No, boy. Pancakes and eggs ain't for dinner."

Benny goes to whining. In a minute he'll be crying, and the boy cries so loud you can hear him clear on up to the third floor. I know, because one day I was up there visiting my friend Laura Lee Flowers and that was the day Mama was trying to give Benny a bath. He was hollering like nobody's business. I don't want to hear that kind of hollering tonight. So I go on ahead and make him the pancakes and eggs, which he wolfs right down.

"Girl, what kind of dinner is this here?"

I didn't hear Mama come in. I believe she does that on purpose, tips up on me trying to catch me in something.

"Mama! Mama! Mama!" Benny jumps up out of his chair and hurls himself at her. It's so embarassing to see him turn into a puppy dog the minute she gets home.

"Boy, get off of me. I'm tired." She pushes him away, steady grumbling at me. "Hard as I work out there trying to keep a roof over your head and clothes on your back, I got to come home to pancakes and eggs for dinner. Girl, you ain't got the sense God gave a ant."

You see there? No hello, no "how you doing, good to see you." Just walk in the door and jump right on my case.

"I fixed it because Benny begged me and I didn't want to hear him crying. If you want me to I'll fix you something else."

"Well, fry me a hot dog or something. And move your lessons off the kitchen table, or they get all nasty."

Mama calls everything I write down 'lessons.' I guess she can't understand why somebody would be writing unless a teacher was making them do it. I don't think I ever seen her write so much as a postcard.

Anyway, she moves my blessings and curses lists to the top of the refrigerator, then sits down and takes her shoes off. She gives a low little moan, like a cat outside in winter, ain't got no place to go.

"You sure look tired, Mama." She wouldn't be such a bad old chick if she wasn't so damned evil all the time.

"Lord knows I am." Talking about how hard she has it and how bad she feels is one of Mama's favorite subjects. She's the world's oldest young woman, that's what Miss Flowers says. "Tired all in my bones. Don't know how I'm going to make it over to the Willises tonight."

"You ain't going over there again! This is going to make three nights in a row."

"I got to work, girl."

"Aw, *Mama.*"

"Aw, *Mama,*" Benny repeats, saying it just like I did.

"Why you always got to repeat what I say, you old simple-minded boy?"

Next thing you know, Benny is crying and Mama has reached over and popped me upside the head.

"See, now. You got your brother to crying. Why you be

such a evil little old gal?"

Because I'm my mother's daughter, I want to tell her. But know better than fixing my mouth to say such a thing, unless I want to get smacked in it. It always be the same thing, every time Mama comes home. She makes me mad, I take it out on Benny, Mama gets mad at me. One of these days I'm going to keep my mouth shut and the whole thing won't never get started.

Mama be the workingest poor woman I ever seen. The way she stays gone, we ought to be millionaires by now. Working all day in the hospital laundry. Working half her nights babysitting some senile old man for a white family in Rolling Meadows. Works all day Sunday at church and that don't pay a penny. Always working and don't never have no money. Always talking about how she puts food on the table and clothes on our back, when it don't be nothing but beans, hot dogs, and Good Will.

Look at Miss Flowers, Laura Lee's mother. She don't need to work. She got her welfare check and her boyfriends. Plus she sells a little reefer on the side. And she stays sharp. None of those old Salvation Army rags Mama be wearing. This lady knows how to dress: high heels, bell-bottom blue jeans, earrings made out of real 10-karat gold. She even got a fur coat one of her boyfriends gave her. You don't see her out work, work, working for nothing. She be at home with her kids, taking it easy and spending time with her boyfriends. Miss Flowers, she knows how to live.

After Mama leaves, I put Benny in front of the TV with a box of Ritz crackers, and I go on up the back stairs to see what Laura Lee and them doing. Their back door is wide open. They're all sitting around the kitchen table, talking and rolling reefers two to a plastic bag. Miss Flowers sells them a dollar a pack. Laura Lee and Miss Flower's sister Chartrice are up there helping her.

"You sure this ain't oregano?" Chartrice sniffs a handful of the stuff. "This shit looking mighty green to be herb."

"Girl, shut up talking and go get me some more plastic bags."

"What do I look like, Steppin Fetchit?" Chartrice keeps poking around in the green stuff piled in the center of the table." I ought to report you to the Better Business Bureau. These tea leaves ain't going to get nobody high."

"Don't worry. If the herb don't give them a buzz, then this will." Miss Flowers takes the reefer she just rolled up and gives it a long lick. Everybody laughs, including me standing outside the unlocked screen door. Chartrice jumps nervously.

"Mae, you need to keep that back door shut. Ain't no telling who might be coming up those back stairs."

"That's just my girl, Little Miss Mae. Mae ain't no heat, is you honey? Come on in. Take a load off."

Miss Flowers is just about the only thing that keeps me from hating my first name too much. We both got the same one; Freddie Mae. Just about as country as you can get.

"And don't you tell nobody, hear?" Miss Flowers had warned me. "Far as the world knows, I'm just Mae. Mae Flowers, like the ones April showers bring."

I sit down. Laura Lee tries to teach me how to roll, but I'm not catching on too good. She also tries to get me into some side chitchat about people at her school I don't even know. But I rather hear the woman talk.

Aretha Franklin is playing on a radio that's always teetering on the back of the stove but never seems to fall off. Miss Flowers sings along.

*"A woman's only human,
this you must understand.
She's not just a plaything,
she's flesh and blood just like a man.*

*If you want a do-right
all day woman,
you got to be a do-right
all night man..."*

"Sing it, Retha! I ain't nothing but a man's woman, got to have me a do-right brother all night long. If I don't get it regular, I gets evil."

"You a man's woman, huh? Then why you ain't never got married to one?" That was Chartrice.

"Damned if I know. It sure would have been convenient."

"Convenient?"

"Hell, yes. Be getting it every night, right on the money." Miss Flowers snaps her fingers.

"Girl, you a mess." Chartrice is laughing so hard all the herb falls out of the reefer she's rolling. "Marriage don't guarantee you getting nothing every night but a hard way to go, and a hard row to hoe."

"Honey, if Joe Junior ain't doing you right, what's the sense in singing the blues? If he don't want it, somebody out there do. Maybe a couple of somebodies."

Chartrice gives a little sneaky smile and a little wave of the reefer stick.

"Honey, hush." Miss Flowers narrows her eyes at her sister. "Don't tell me somebody got her a backdoor man. Do tell, sister. Do tell."

Chartrice rolls her eyes at me and Laura Lee, sitting there with our eyes and ears wide open. Miss Flowers takes the cue.

"Come on, girls. Get getting. This is grown folks talk."

I make my relectant way to Laura Lee's bedroom, the conversation still on my mind.

"Laura Lee, what was your Mama and them talking about?"

Laura Lee isn't too much interested. I guess she's heard it all before.

"Doing it."

"Doing what?"

"You know." Laura Lee makes an 'O' with her thumb and forefinger, then sticks another finger through it. "The P.U.S.S.Y."

I've heard the word before. But I'm still not quite sure what it is.

"How do they do it?"

"You mean you don't know about the P.U.S.S.Y.?" She draws herself up like our old fourth grade teacher, Miss Caruso, used to do before she gave a lecture on the digestive system. "That's when a boy takes his thing and puts it in your tee-tee hole. If he puts it all the way in, that's the P.U.S.S.Y. If he don't, it's just playing."

"Girl, you a lie. He puts that big old thing in you? That must really hurt."

Laura turns down the corners of her mouth and shakes her head.

"Naw, it don't hurt much."

"How do you know? Don't mean to tell me you did it before."

Laura shrugs like it ain't nothing.

"One time. With Junebug Wilson."

"You did? What was it like? Tell me, girl."

Laura shook her head.

"Ain't nothing to tell. I don't see why they make such a big thing about it. It ain't much fun."

By the time I graduated from grammar school, Laura Lee had dropped out six months before, pregnant with her first baby. She said when her mother found out about it, she beat her butt so bad she couldn't sit down for a whole week. But what I want to know is this; if it wasn't no fun, how come Laura got interested enough to do it again with Junebug? I don't think she was telling me the whole story.

This P.U.S.S.Y. business. It seems to be a secret everyone knows about but me. Like once you do it, you're in a special club and can't tell anyone else the password. Mama's a member.

"Don't be talking that filth at my kitchen table." When I ask her to explain the subject to me, she reaches over and slaps the shit out of me. "I don't know where you be getting this mess from. Yes, I do. It's Laura and that old whorish Mama of her'n. That girl ain't even thirteen good and she already having a baby. You stay away from up there, hear me?"

Yep, she's in on it. Mama found herself somebody to do with in her bed the filth she don't want me talking about at the kitchen table.

Out of all the available men on the Southside of Chicago, you would think that Mama could do better for herself than Otis Clemmons. First, he's twenty years older than Mama if he's a day. Second, he's one of those high-yellow dudes with wavy hair, act like somebody supposed to bow down in front of him because of it. Third, he don't do nothing but sit up and drink beer, complain about his bad back, and try to boss somebody around like he their daddy. Which he ain't. Otis Clemmons is definitely going on my curses list.

He starts spending nights up in Mama's room. She brings him in late, when she thinks we're sleeping. Benny be snoring back. But I be hearing everything that goes on in this house. The first night it was such a scrambling and a rattling on the other side of our bedroom wall, I'm thinking we got rats in the house. Until I hear my Mama hollering.

"Lordy! Whoa, Lordy, sweet Jesus!"

Like it's the Lord doing it to her instead of that old slick-headed Otis. Before I know it, Sweet Jesus Otis is up here living with us. With his old stanky feet, bad breath self. Go up in the bathroom, stay in there a whole hour. Miss Flowers says that this is because he is full of shit.

"Full of shit and fake as a three dollar bill. Always bragging about how his Mama's a full-blooded Indian, when you and me both know his Mama's as black as the ace of spades and his daddy was an old white man she picked up off Skid Row. Plus, I hear he's a minute man."

"What's a minute man?"

Miss Flowers laughs deep in her throat. That 'I know a Sweet Jesus secret' laugh.

"Never mind about that."

I figure it out for myself. But I don't know about that. The bed on the other side of the wall seems to rattle much more than a minute most nights.

Once Otis gets in here, he tries to boss us all around. Be telling my mother what to wear, how to fix her hair. Wouldn't be so bad if he got her to looking good. He just don't want Mama going outdoors with nothing showing, that's his thing. If he could wrap Mama up in one of those things they wear overseas, the women don't have nothing showing but their eyes, old Otis Clemmons would do it in a minute.

"Girl, cover up your bust. And put a coat on. I can't stand these niggers looking all down my woman's dress."

He tries to control me and Benny too. Well, Benny don't too much care about it, as long as he gets his TV and his something to eat. I told you he was retarded, right? But he's not ill-formed or nothing. He ain't got those bugged out, slanty eyes like some of those kids go to his school. He don't be dribbling spit out his mouth or nothing like that. He's just like a big old baby. And he don't bother nobody, long as you leave him be. But Otis Clemmons won't. That would be too much like right.

"Boy, you watches too much TV. Turn that thing off. And pick up all that popcorn off the floor." I guess Benny's not moving fast enough for him. He points a long yellow finger at him and hollers: "Do it!"

"Do it!" Benny looks up and points his brown finger back at him.

"Don't you mock me, fool. I'm a dangerous nigger."

He's dangerous all right. He ain't been here but six months when he has Mama sending Benny off to some home for the 'profoundly retarded' in St. Charles. I'll never forget how Benny cries when we leave him there. And I'll never forgive Otis for making Mama do it.

With Benny out of the way, he starts in on me. First, he won't let me watch nothing I want to on TV.

"Peyton Place? What kind of trash is that for a young girl to be looking at?"

Then he starts trying to do me like he does Mama. Criticizing what I be wearing.

"You wearing that sleeveless blouse? To church? Go pull that thing off and put on you some *clothes.*"

When I start to sprout titties it really gives him the blues. One weekend when Benny's out of his jail visiting home, I decide to give him a bath. He don't be too clean since he been up in St. Charles. Seems like I've been washing Benny up all my life. It's not that hard to do, as long as you do it a certain way. Get lots of bubbles in there for him to play with. Soap him up everywhere but his face. He hates getting soap in his eyes. And let him splash all he wants. He loves to splash. By the time we finish, I'm just as wet as he is.

I go to Mama's room to get me a towel. As usual, Otis is sitting up there drinking. He looks at me real hard in my wet tee-shirt.

"What the hell is the matter with you?" A red-eyed devil. "Parading around in front of me like that."

I just ignore him, searching for the towel. He keeps at me.

"Why ain't you got no bra on?"

"I ain't got one."

"Then get you one."

"With what? You got the money for me to buy it with?"

He clamps his red mouth shut then. With his cheap self. He ain't hardly got it to buy beer for his sorry gut, let alone buy me a bra.

He must have talked to Mama about it though. Next Saturday morning she takes me downtown on the El. I don't know where we're going until we get there: the Foundations Department at Montgomery Wards. She buys me two training bras, cost $12.50.

But after the bras, it's something else. It's going to always be something else. I'm wearing hot pants one day because it's hot. That's why they call them hot pants, you wear them when it's hot. It's ninety-eight degrees outside and I'm cooking biscuits inside. Sweat is running off me like rain.

Otis comes up in the kitchen, gets him a beer, and sits down. Hot as hell in that kitchen, he come sitting down where I'm at. Y'all *know* he wants to start something. I pass by him going to put the Crisco back in the pantry.

"Girl, if you don't get your black tail out of my face, you better."

See, you're not supposed to mess with people when it's ninety-eight degrees. Especially when they're baking biscuits in a hot kitchen.

"Leave me alone." That all I say. That's all I want.

"Are you talking back to me, little evil gal?"

"What do it sound like to you?"

Otis halfway chokes on his beer.

"Is you lost your mind? Back talking me and swishing you little naked ass around this kitchen."

"Ain't none of your kitchen. Ain't none of your ass either."

Otis wipes the beer from his mustache.

"Bitch." He hisses the word between his teeth, like an old yellow snake. Ain't nobody never called me that word. "You better get your butt out of here before I beat it for you. Got your little ass hanging out like you think somebody want to look at it."

"You can look all you want." I'd give him his 'bitch.' "Because you damn sure ain't getting none."

Miss Flowers had cussed a man out like that in a tavern one night. She said the man's mouth had dropped all the way down to the floor, he couldn't think of nothing to say back. Otis' red mouth does the exact same thing. And I walk right out the back door. Let the biscuits burn.

But Otis Clemmons is a dangerous nigger. I overhear them on the other side of the wall. The bed's not rattling tonight. They in there talking in hard whispers.

"Eddie Mae, that girl is running too fast, too young."

"She ain't that bad, Otis."

"She is ruint. Won't be but a matter of time before she come up pregnant like her friend upstairs. Then what you going to say? 'She ain't that bad?' That child is rotten. She needs more discipline than she's getting in this house."

"But, Otis. A place like that?"

"Would do her a world of good. She need to learn she can't run over everybody like she runs over you."

So that's what it is. Get rid of us so he can have Mama all to himself. All the little bit of love she can squeeze up, his love. All the little bit of time she has, his time. All her little bit of money, his money. But I ain't nobody's Benny to be sent off to jail crying. I'd sooner run away than let him send me somewhere like St. Charles. And I do.

First I go down to Phoenix, Illinois where I got some cousins who don't really want me there. Then to Chartrice, Miss Flowers sister, who works me like a dog: cooking, babysitting, cleaning up after her and her nine nasty kids.

Mama catches up with me after about three weeks. One of Chartrice's kids lets her in the house. She comes tipping in like a guest not sure of her welcome. She sits on the far edge of the plastic-covered couch while I sweep up the front room floor.

"How you doing, baby? You all right?"

Mama hasn't called me baby in so long, it makes me feel like crying. But it's not me, it's her that starts it up. The first time I can ever remember seeing Mama with tears on her face. And I can't help but blame Otis for putting them there.

"I'm sorry, Mama. But I just couldn't sit there and let Otis send me off to some home for bad girls. I ain't done nothing wrong."

"Baby, what I'm going to do with you? I tried my best to raise you up right. But I ain't done such a good job. I guess I ain't no kind of mother."

"You are so. You're a great mother. It's Otis who's the problem."

Mama acts like she don't even hear me talking.

"I stay gone so much, working. You having to stay home with Benny all the time. That's a lot to put on a young girl."

"I don't mind, Mama. Benny ain't been much trouble."

"You getting to be a young woman now. And I don't know how to protect you no more. It's all kinds of dogs and rats out there walking around on two legs. Some of them would just love to get ahold a young girl like you and use her for toilet paper."

"Mama, we never did have no problems in our family until a year ago. We were happy until Otis came along."

She hears me that time. And it don't do nothing but make her mad.

"Otis Clemmons is a good man! He treats you like a daughter. It ain't every man would take up with a woman with two kids and treat them like they was his own. And instead of praising the Lord for him, you act like Ugly was your middle name. Back-talking. Chasing up behind boys. Stealing. Running away. Otis ain't doing nothing but trying to help you, baby. He don't want to see your fresh life wasted before you even start living it. He don't want to see you go wrong."

No, he don't want to see me go wrong. He just wants to see me go away. And he gets his wish.

I didn't tell you about the stealing, right? Okay, I stole some things. I stole some clothes. It wasn't my fault. First of all, Mama and them don't never buy me nothing. Especially since Otis been laying up there mooching off of her. I'll be starting high school this fall. What I'm going to look like walking up in high school in those old mammy-made thrift store rags Mama makes me wear? They don't be fitting. They way out of style.

Occasionally Mama gives me something halfway nice.

"Here, girl. This blouse don't fit me no more. You might as well take it."

Problem is, something Mama's outgrown or got from the white folks' house would still be two sizes too big for me. And won't hardly be high fashion. I'm just tired of looking patched together, like somebody's little ragamuffin. I want to wear things that come with the tags still attached. I want things picked out with me in mind. I want things that nobody else has worn before me. So I rip them off.

Only thing I can remember that was bought for me brand new is those two training bras. And even those didn't fit right. Mama bought them big, for me to grow into. But ain't no telling when I'm going to grow titties that big. So I have to steal me some more.

The only problem with stealing stuff is that I get caught. I'm not even in the store or nothing. I'm out on the street looking inside my windbreaker to see what all I got out with, when this cop comes up and asks me where are my receipts. Ain't nobody there but Otis when they call home, so he has to come down to the station and get me.

And then the Leslie thing. It's not fair. Mama and them swear up and down that I'm trying to do the Sweet Jesus with Laura Lee's older brother.

How Leslie Flowers got in that family, I'll never know. Otis says Miss Flowers went up to the north side and did it with a Puerto Rican. Old Otis got his nerve. At least Leslie don't look like he got yellow fever. He's nice and beige, like the inside part of a loaf of whole wheat bread. Of course, Laura Lee and Miss Flowers look more like the crust.

I'll admit that I do love me some Leslie Flowers. He is *too* cute, looks just like Smokey Robinson. But Leslie ain't hardly thinking about me. Sometimes he'll call out, "Hey, Skinny Minnie" when he sees me over there visiting Laura, or alone out on the street. I think it's because he can't remember my name. Once he kisses me, but it's not a serious 'in love' kiss. It's more like he's kissing me off. Because Leslie Flowers is the kind of boy that girls go to him, not the other way around. He's got plenty of women, Miss Flowers says, who love to give it up.

Remember how Laura got her butt beat when she turned up pregnant? When she finds out one of Leslie's girlfriends is pregnant, Miss Flowers act like she proud of it.

"Well, at least the boy can make a baby." She flicks her cigarette ash into the cup of her hand. "Long as they don't be bringing it around here for me to watch."

See, Mama and Otis don't hardly have to worry about me turning up pregnant. As much as I love me some Leslie, I ain't hardly going to let something in me that (don't care what Laura Lee says) must hurt like a tooth getting pulled. And then to have a baby on top of it? Not me. I know from taking care of Benny all these years that a baby ain't no kind of fun.

But Mama and Otis, they don't believe me. They know the secret password of the Sweet Jesus Club and think I must know it too.

So Otis gets his way. He has Mama take me down to the station. This train is taking me off to what kind of jail, I'm not really sure. I'm on my way, and out of his. Him and Mama free to make that bed talk as loud as it can while I'm gone.

Sitting here watching the Southside of Chicago disappear behind me, I can't think of a single thing to go on my blessings list. Everything is a curse. Don't nobody pay attention to me, don't nobody want to hear my side of it. But you know what? I'm going to make them listen.

I'm writing it down. I'm writing it all down, the whole story. And when I finish I'm sending it to Otis Clemmons so he can see himself, and Mama so she can see herself in it. She don't have to fret about sombody using me. She needs to be worrying more about herself. See, I ain't never going to get as turned around behind some no-account man as Mama is with Otis. I ain't about to make a man my religion. Or be used as nobody's roll of toilet paper.

And another thing. Yeah, I'm riding this trian. But you think I'm going to set back and let the bars close behind me? When I know how to get up and walk? Not hardly.

I may be going away, but I'm sure not staying.

The South Side: A Brief History

Dominic Pacyga

Chicago grew up on the South Side. The first major neighborhoods appeared south of the river and the emerging Loop. It was on the South Side that Chicago found its soul amidst the packinghouses, steel mills, balloon-frame tenements and storefronts of the "numbered streets" that stretch below Roosevelt Road and away from the lake. Here Chicago made money off of the bountiful natural resources of the Midwest and West, and out of the sweat of cheap immigrant and African American labor. The money moved on and left behind some of the most spirited white ethnic, Hispanic, and African American neighborhoods in urban America.

The South Side has always been a place of stark and often amusing contrasts. Elegant lakefront mansions in the old Prairie Avenue District or in Kenwood, Hyde Park, or South Shore stood only minutes away from some of the meanest immigrant and black neighborhoods in the world. Upton Sinclair, James T. Farrell and Richard Wright explored those areas in their fiction and set an example for others to write urban fiction. A great university settled in along the lakefront at the same time that the razzle and dazzle of the Columbian Exposition turned the University of Chicago's front yard into a carnival along the Midway Plaisance, giving the term midway to every amusement park, county fair, and circus that followed. On South Side streets African American English mixes with Polish, Serbo-Croatian, Czech, German, Chinese, Spanish, Arabic, and countless other languages and dialects. Polish mountaineers built a Tatra Mountain chalet on Archer Avenue just minutes from the Chinatown Gate, the Balzekas Museum of Lithuanian Culture, and the DuSable Museum of African American Culture; while the Irish maintain their heritage in Beverly, Canaryville, and Bridgeport. Gothic church and synagogue steeples and onion domes pierce the sky vying for dominance with smokestacks, railroad bridges, granaries, and power lines. They are joined by Black Muslim and Palestinian mosques. Everywhere diversity shows its Janus-like face of tradition and change along the South Side streets.

That is not to say that this variety has always meant a peaceful diversity either now or in the past. Racial, ethnic, and class battles have occurred regularly on the South Side. In the nineteenth century clashes occurred between the Bridgeport Irish and Germans. Later Poles and Lithuanians fought along Morgan Street and in Back of the Yards. Labor strikes in the stockyards and steel mills often resulted in violence. Hyde Park area homes frequently were built with steel enforced rooms in case the working class ever came visiting to revenge itself upon the upper classes living along the lakefront.

All of these conflicts, however, paled before the race riot that shook Chicago in July of 1919. During that terrible summer week, thirty-eight died and several hundred were injured, primarily on the South Side. Gangs roamed freely attacking often innocent bystanders until the Illinois State Militia finally separated the races. That riot set in stone race relations in Chicago for the rest of the century, and made permanent the tradition of segregation, temporary integration, and resegregation that has plagued the South Side ever since.

Still in the spirit of contrasts the South Side continues to surprise. Hyde Park today remains the nation's largest integrated neighborhood, while Beverly and Morgan Park to the southwest continue their noble experiment in integration. Even Marquette Park, known nationally for racial clashes from the time that Dr. Martin Luther King, Jr., led an open housing march there in 1966, is integrated, and has been for about ten years. The future of that attempt at diversity, and of the important work of the Southwest Catholic Cluster Project which is trying to break the old habit of resegregation on the South Side, is still in question. Racial conflicts and hate crimes still occur among the bungalows and two-flats of South Side streets. Other kinds of violence do too as the terrible murder rate in Englewood and other South Side neighborhoods attests. Drugs, gangs, and cruelty rule too many American urban streets. It should not be surprising that the same South Side streets once ruled by white ethnic gangs, such as Ragan's Colts, and by Al Capone's men are still controlled by brutality.

The stereotype of the South Side as the "poor side" or the "shot and beer" side of town that is filled with ghetto blacks and racist whites is, however, not true. Like all such simplifications this one misses the point of the South Side experience. To deny the reality of poverty and racism would be silly. The shadow of the Stateway Gardens and Robert Taylor Homes, which together make up a nightmare of modernist architecture gone mad and are the longest housing projects in the world, attest to that fact. Still the quiet elegant streets of Black Chatham and the vibrant streets of Spanish, Black, and East European Back of the Yards or Polish, Lithuanian and Hispanic Brighton Park or the Arab merchants on West 63rd Street tell a different story. It is a success story, a very American story even in its excesses and tragedies.

The South Side made the city a dynamic and diverse place. In turn the city has often paid back the South Side by ignoring it. It is hard to be a South Sider in a North Side town. The life of a South Sider can be a frustrating one to say the least. Even the current Mayor Daley who lives within walking distance of the new Comiskey Park has admitted to being a Cub fan! One hopes that this is simply a shrewd political ploy to reach out to a citywide constituency. The South Side does not get a lot of respect from the media or from other Chicagoans, especially North Siders or suburbanites. Indeed one gets the feeling that most media types live in those other God forsaken places beyond the boundaries of White Sox Country. That they do not visit the South Side frequently is obvious.

Now 1919 is a year etched in the collective memory of the city because of the riot, but also because of the Black Sox scandal (not to mention the Great Steel Strike). The White Sox indeed seemed to be under a curse ever since that fateful day when eight of their players fell victim to sin. For forty years, through five Cub pennants (but alas, no World Series crowns) and countless Yankee championships, the White Sox bumbled their way through major league season after major league season.

Finally relief came in 1959, and the original Mayor Daley (a Sox fan) set off the air raid sirens to celebrate a Sox pennant and to scare Cub fans who thought that Soviet bombers were zeroing in on their ivy-covered world. By the way it was a South Sider, Bill Veeck, who put that ivy on the Cub walls back when his father ran that organization. Happiness filled the South Side in those days when Chicagoans danced in the streets instead of looting after a victory. Happiness reigned supreme when the White Sox vanquished the Los Angeles Dodgers in the first game of the World Series by a very Un-White Sox score of 11 to 1. The Dodgers, however, who had recently abandoned a place much like the South Side for the West Coast, prevailed; and the Sox have not seen a World Series since. It was long ago, but hope reigns even more supreme than does happiness in a true South Side heart. We may not be happy, but we are hopeful.

Nineteen Fifty-Nine was a good year for Midway Airport too. It was the world's busiest airport, and it stood proud on the South Side. A South Side that still boasted the largest stockyards in the world and vast steel mills. A South Side that had provided a home for the city's mayors from 1933 on, and also had its own National Football League franchise in the Cardinals. The Bears played up in Wrigley Field. The Sox loss to the Dodgers was the beginning of a slide from grace. Soon the Cardinals were playing even farther south in St. Louis and then eventually in Phoenix. The packinghouses closed, and then in 1971 the stockyards disappeared completely after processing over one billion head of livestock. Chicago lost more than its pervasive smell. The International Amphitheater gave way to McCormick Place and the Rosemont Horizon. O'Hare Airport opened and Midway Airport turned into a ghost town. The steel mills closed down and you could suddenly breathe the air in South Chicago and South Deering. White flight and later African American flight to the suburbs depleted the middle class, and made those who stayed behind more nervous. The city lost nearly 500,000 industrial jobs in the forty-five years after World War II. Most of these disappeared from the South Side. The Black, White and Hispanic working class suddenly saw investment dry up and blow away to the suburbs or the Sunbelt. Sixty-third Street from Stoney Island to Halsted had once been the "bright lights" district of the city. At 63rd and Halsted a huge neighborhood shopping district rivaled even the Loop. Suddenly the old strips were vacant. The shops boarded up. City stores could not compete with shopping malls like Evergreen Plaza and River Oaks or even the in-city Ford City, built on the remains of Chicago's wartime industrial might. When Bridgeport's Michael Bilandic lost to Jane Byrne in that strange snow-cursed election it seemed that another nail had been hammered into the South Side's coffin. Still hope reigns eternal.

Harold Washington, Gene Sawyer and the current Daley returned the political crown to the South Side. In politics South Siders, Black and White, play like the old New York Yankees. They play to win. Ask Michael J. Madigan, king of the 13th Ward and the Illinois House of Representatives. De La Salle Institute, school to five mayors, the late Cook County Board President Dan Ryan, and more politicians and community leaders than just about anyplace else in the country sits just a few blocks east of that temple of doom, Comiskey Park. It is in this high school that Chicago politics played South Side style was born and nourished. Maybe it is this game that South Siders play the best.

In part it was the game of politics that gave Chicago its first new baseball stadium since 1916 and kept the White Sox in Chicago. In April 1991 the White Sox opened the new Comiskey Park by losing big. The frustration continues, but in a new ballpark, and unlike the football Cardinals the Sox have stayed on the South Side. Midway Airport has also been brought back from the dead. It almost died again, but is holding on as politicians play their games over the future of air travel in Illinois. While the stockyards are gone forever, the site of the old cattle, hog, sheep, and horse pens is seeing a slight industrial rebirth. Suddenly even old Bridgeport looks somewhat fashionable as development spreads south of the Loop through Dearborn Park down to 14th and State Street where $500,000 single-family mansions are being erected on the site of the abandoned Santa Fe yards. Chinatown too is spreading in every direction as Hong Kong money searches for investment in the West. A new rapid transit line is making its way along the underused railroad corridor that once served the stockyards and the southwest industrial belt. The new line is starting to attract the attention of investors to the neighborhoods southwest of downtown. Mexicans and other Latino groups are filling in the spaces being abandoned by the Poles, Germans, Irish, Lithuanians and Slovaks of another generation. Rebirth goes on, hope springs eternal, and change is a constant even on the "shot and beer" side of town.

In the end the South Side is Chicago. It is here where the city faces its biggest problems: racial conflict, gangs, violence, drugs, deindustrialization, poor schools, bad housing. It is also here where the future of the city is being worked out by men and women who want to stay in the city. There is opportunity here, the opportunity to build a new city. That is the hope beyond all the frustration. It is hard being a South Sider in a North Side city, but most of us wouldn't have it any other way.

Contributors' Notes

ASA BABER is a contributing editor to *Playboy Magazine*. A collection of his recent columns is available from Birch Lane Press and is titled *Naked At Gender Gap: A Man's View of the War Between the Sexes*. He is the author of the novel *The Land of a Million Elephants* (Morrow), has published dozens of stories in publications ranging from *Chicago Magazine* to *TriQuarterly*. He's also made guest appearances on numerous TV shows including *48 Hours* (CBS), *The Today Show* (NBC), *Crossfire* (CNN), *The Oprah Winfrey Show* (ABC) and *John McLaughlin's One on One* (PBS).

ROSE BLOUIN is a photographer and professor of English at Columbia College. Her photography has appeared in may exhibitions throughout the U.S. She lives on the South Side with her two children.

STUART DYBEK is a widely published author, with works appearing in many anthologies and publications including *Ploughshares*, *Chicago Magazine* and *Seattle Review*. His collections of short stories, *The Coast of Chicago* (Knopf) and *Brass Knuckles* (University of Pittsburgh Press), have received numerous awards. He is a professor of English at Western Michigan University.

HAROLD HOLT, born in Chicago in 1966, is a graduate of Columbia College Chicago and is a fiction writer and poet currently teaching at Harold Washington College.

ANGELA JACKSON was born in Greenville, Mississippi, but moved to Chicago at an early age. The fifth of nine children, she lived on the South Side in the same house until she left for college. Educated at Northwestern and the University of Chicago, she credits the community-based OBAC (Organization of Black American Culture) Writers Workshop under Hoyt W. Fuller with her early development as a writer. Other credits she gives to her mother, who was an avid reader, and a father who was an accomplished storyteller and amateur blues lyricist. Jackson has published poetry and fiction in a number of journals, including *Black World*, *Nommo*, *Essence*, *Yellow Silk*, *Black American Lietature Forum*, *Tri-Quarterly*, *StoryQuarterly*, *Chicago Review*, and *Callaloo*. The best of her several collections of poetry appear in *And All These Roads Be Luminous* (Third World Press, 1991). Jackson is the winner of numerous awards, including the Pushcart Prize for Poetry, 1989; NEA and Illinois Arts Council (IAC) Fellowships in 1979 and 1980; IAC Literary Awards for Fiction, and the Hoyt W. Fuller Award for Literary Excellence from the DuSable Museum.

SANDRA JACKSON-OPOKU is a poet, journalist and fiction writer, born in 1950's Chicago in a South Side neighborhood called 'Bronzeville'. *Sweet Jesus Club* is excerpted from *Songs and Daughters*, a forthcoming novel for which she has won a National Endowment for the Arts Literary Fellowship, a CCLM/General Electric Fiction Award for Young Writers, an Illinois Arts Council Completion Grant and Finalist Award, and the Ragdale Foundation U.S.-African Writers Fellowship.

ARLENE GREENE is a native Chicagoan and has lived in various South and North Side neighborhoods. She has an M.A. in English Literature from Roosevelt College. She teaches literature at Columbia College Chicago and serves as a Tutor Advisor at the Montgomery Ward/Cabrini-Green Tutoring project. Her fiction has appeared in *Perihelion*, *Hair Trigger IV & V* and *Best of Hair Trigger*, and her poetry has appeared in *Oyez Review*. She is currently working on a novel. She has a daughter, four sons, two grandsons and now resides in Skokie with her husband Barry and their three cats.

MICHAEL FITZGERALD currently works as a senior writer for *Computerworld*, a trade publication. He lived in Chicago for ten years before moving to Massachusetts in 1991. This is his first short story.